J.T. EDSON'S
FLOATING OUTFIT

The toughest bunch of Rebels that ever lost a war, they fought for the South, and then for Texas, as the legendary Floating Outfit of "Ole Devil" Hardin's O.D. Connected Ranch.

MARK COUNTER was the best-dressed man in the West: always dressed fit-to-kill. **BELLE BOYD** was as deadly as she was beautiful, with a "Manhattan" model Colt tucked under her long skirts. **THE YSABEL KID** was Comanche fast and Texas tough. And the most famous of them all was **DUSTY FOG**, the ex-cavalryman known as the Rio Hondo Gun Wizard.

J. T. Edson has captured all the excitement and adventure of the raw frontier in this magnificent Western series. Turn the page for a complete list of Berkley Floating Outfit titles.

J. T. EDSON'S
FLOATING OUTFIT
WESTERN ADVENTURES
FROM BERKLEY

THE YSABEL KID	THE LAW OF THE GUN
SET TEXAS BACK ON HER FEET	THE PEACEMAKERS
THE HIDE AND TALLOW MEN	THE RUSHERS
TROUBLED RANGE	THE QUEST FOR BOWIE'S BLADE
SIDEWINDER	THE FORTUNE HUNTERS
McGRAW'S INHERITANCE	THE TEXAN
THE BAD BUNCH	THE RIO HONDO KID
TO ARMS, TO ARMS, IN DIXIE!	RIO GUNS
HELL IN THE PALO DURO	GUN WIZARD
GO BACK TO HELL	TRIGGER FAST
THE SOUTH WILL RISE AGAIN	RETURN TO BACKSIGHT
.44 CALIBER MAN	THE MAKING OF A LAWMAN
A HORSE CALLED MOGOLLON	TERROR VALLEY
GOODNIGHT'S DREAM	APACHE RAMPAGE
FROM HIDE AND HORN	THE RIO HONDO WAR
THE HOODED RIDERS	THE FLOATING OUTFIT
QUIET TOWN	THE MAN FROM TEXAS
TRAIL BOSS	GUNSMOKE THUNDER
WAGONS TO BACKSIGHT	THE SMALL TEXAN
RANGELAND HERCULES	THE TOWN TAMERS
THE HALF BREED	WHITE INDIANS
THE WILDCATS	OLD MOCCASINS ON THE TRAIL
THE FAST GUNS	WACO'S DEBT
GUNS IN THE NIGHT	THE HARD RIDERS
CUCHILO	THE GENTLE GIANT
A TOWN CALLED YELLOWDOG	THE TRIGGER MASTER
THE TROUBLE BUSTERS	

J.T. Edson

THE TRIGGER MASTER

BERKLEY BOOKS, NEW YORK

Originally published in Great Britain as
MASTER OF TRIGGERNOMETRY
This Berkley book contains the complete
text of the original edition.
It has been completely reset in a typeface
designed for easy reading and was printed
from new film.

THE TRIGGER MASTER

A Berkley Book/published by arrangement with
Transworld Publishers Ltd.

PRINTING HISTORY
Corgi edition published 1981
Berkley edition/July 1986

ISBN: 0-425-09087-6

A BERKLEY BOOK® TM 757,375
Berkley Books are published by The Berkley Publishing Group,
200 Madison Avenue, New York, NY 10016.
The name "BERKLEY" and the stylized "B"
with design are trademarks belonging to
Berkley Publishing Corporation.

PRINTED IN THE UNITED STATES OF AMERICA

For Eugene Cunningham,
whose book, *Triggernometry*,
has been a great source
of information and interest.

Author's Note

Although some of the events recorded herein first appeared as, Part One, "Dusty Fog in The Schoolteacher," THE HARD RIDERS, we did not have access to the full details at that time. These have now been made available to us by Alvin Dustine "Cap" Fog, together with permission to reproduce them.

As usual, to save our "old hands" from repetition and for the benefit of new readers, we are giving details of the background and special qualifications of Captain Dustine Edward Marsden "Dusty" Fog in an Appendix.

We realize that, in our present "permissive" society, we could include the actual profanities used by various people, but we do not concede that a spurious desire to create "realism" is a valid reason to do so. Lastly, as we do not conform to the current "trendy" pandering to the exponents of the metric system, we will continue to employ pounds, ounces, miles, yards, feet and inches where weights and distances are concerned, except when referring to the calibres of such weapons as are gauged in millimetres.

J. T. Edson
Active member, Western Writers of America,
Melton Mowbray, England.

THE TRIGGER MASTER

CHAPTER ONE

That's Faster Than the Prince

"Hey now!" Walter "Trader" Staines ejaculated, remembering just in time to speak in a whisper, despite the surprise he had just received, as he and his companion crouched among the bushes and watched, from the concealment of the foliage, two of the men in the bottom of the valley removing the covers from the horse which they had brought with them. "I've never set eyes on that bay before!"

"I didn't think you would have, Walter," Ezekiel Barnesley answered, equally *sotto voce*. As usual, he refrained from employing the sobriquet by which the other was generally known. His tone and demeanour became charged with warning as he continued, "And we'd better make certain they don't catch us watching it *now*. Mr. Keleney's had it brought in secretly to be run in the race on Saturday, but you won't find it in the stables at his place and it won't be entered under *his* name either when they go to the post." He paused and glanced at the man by his side as if wanting to make sure his point had been understood. Deducing from the way in which the pair of field glasses brought by the other were being raised as an aid to conducting a closer examination, he went on, "What do *you* think of *it*?"

Although there had been fairly heavy rain the previous

night, the weather was now fine and pleasantly warm without having attained sufficient heat to dry out the ground which had received a soaking from the downpour. The valley was on the rolling plains of South-East Texas some three miles west of Grattan, seat of Dale County. However, the attire of the two watchers suggested they followed more sedentary occupations than those who earned a living by working on the open range country. Both had on none too expensive three piece suits, collarless white shirts, derby hats and footwear which, even in the case of Staines—who was the owner of the town's only livery barn—was more satisfactory for walking than riding or driving a wagon.

Of medium height, approaching his fiftieth birthday, Staines was thickset although now running to fat. He had an accent which indicated he had either been born or spent much of his life south of the Mason-Dixon line,[1] if not entirely in the Lone Star State. He had thinning brown hair and the jovial, reddened face of a man who spent much of his time out of doors being pleasant to others. Of late, the horse trading from which he had acquired his nickname had been carried out in or around his place of business instead of him having to go in search of it on the range.

Taller and thinner, although conveying an impression to the contrary, Barnesley was a few years younger than his companion. Long hours spent bending over a desk had bowed his narrow shoulders and he peered short-sightedly as a result of his vision having been impaired by frequently perusing documents with great care in indifferent lighting. Such a way of life had given his sharp features the colour and texture of ancient parchment. He had the seedy and downtrodden air often found in clerks which was enchanced by the whining timbre of his New England manner of speech.[2] He looked like

---

1   *"Mason-Dixon" line: sometimes erroneously called the "Mason-Dixie" line. The boundary between Pennsylvania and Maryland, as surveyed in 1763-67 by the Englishmen, Charles Mason and Jeremiah Dixon, which came to be regarded as the dividing line separating the Southern "Slave" and Northern "Free" States of America. J. T. E.*

2   *"New England": the North-East section of the United States of America, including New Hampshire, Maine, Vermont, Massachusetts, Rhode Island and Connecticut, which was first settled primarily by people from the British Isles. J.T.E.*

others in similar forms of employment, who had grown too old to seek more stimulating work.

"It's not a bad looking critter, I'll admit," Staines assessed, lowering the field glasses at the completion of what had been a lengthy and informative study regardless of being carried out at a distance. As had become second nature to him, he had adopted the almost depreciatory manner of one well versed in the art of purchasing, or exchanging, horses. Nor did the tone entirely depart as he continued, "Thing being, it's *running* and not just *looks* 's wins races. Which we both of us know how good Bull's Black Prince is at doing *that.*"

"We do *indeed!*" Barnesley agreed, with what was remarkable vehemence for him. "And that was why I thought, when I chanced to overhear what was to be done, that it could be worth our while to come out here and see what they are up to."

"It *could* be at that," Staines admitted, still retaining his horse-trader's voice and his gaze was speculative, if not out-and-out suspicious, as he turned it to his companion. "Only I didn't know you went in for anything like betting on horse races, Ezekiel."

"I don't make a *habit* of it, I'll admit," Barnesley conceded. "But neither does Mr. Keleney pay me so munificently that I'm averse to acquiring some extra money by making a wager, providing it can be done without the risk of losing of course."

"And you reckon it can be?"

"I can't *guarantee* it. All I'm sure of, knowing him as I do, is that Mr. Keleney would not be going to all the trouble he has taken to obtain and bring the horse here in secret unless there's a *very* good reason. But I don't know enough about horses to judge for myself, which is why I asked *you* to come and give me your opinion."

"No offense meant, Ezekiel," Barnes claimed in a placatory manner, having caught what he took to be a note of querulous resentment in the clerk's voice while the explanation was being made. "I'm right pleased you told me. Like you say, Bull's not keeping it out of sight just for the sake of its health and finding out what it's capable of could pay off good."

Receiving such an enthusiastic nod that he concluded his

apology was accepted, the owner of the livery barn raised the field glasses once more and resumed his scrutiny.

The horse in the valley, a bay gelding with a white star on the brow and three white stockings, was just under fifteen hands and would weigh about one thousand pounds. Even at the distance which separated it from Staines, its excellent health and physical condition was apparent. Its short head had wide-set, intelligent eyes and open nostrils. Well set on powerful shoulders, the neck was sufficiently muscular to augment the broad and deep chest. Short and firmly muscled, the back had well sprung ribs and strong loins, joining massive and rounded hindquarters. All in all, the effect was that of a compact and exceptionally muscular animal; yet it was neither over bulky, clumsy, or awkward on its feet. However, to the uninitiated—despite being hard, clean, and with short pastens—the legs appeared somewhat finer than might be expected for carrying a body so potentially puissant. Being better informed, by virtue of what was now his secondary trade, Staines regarded them as ideal for their purpose. This was to be able to accelerate quickly from a standing start and transport the rider for a short distance at a great speed.

The possession of such qualities by the gelding accounted for the watchers being hidden and the clerk's warning about the necessity of avoiding any indication being given to their presence.

The bay was intended to compete in a forthcoming race—over a distance of four hundred and forty yards—of the kind which had given its breed the name, "American quarter horse."[3] As it was about to be subjected to a secret trial with

3 *The "American quarter horse," sometimes known as "steeldust," "Billies," or "Shilohs," is the oldest of the breeds developed in what was to become the United States. The strain was commenced, during the early part of the Seventeenth Century, by breeders in Virginia and the Carolinas crossing imported English animals with Arabs, Barbs and Turks brought to the "New World" by the Spaniards. The purpose behind this careful selective breeding was to produce mounts suitable for competition in the popular "Colonial" sports of "match racing," short sprints which usually took place over distances not exceeding a quarter of a mile and so could frequently be run on the street of a village. In addition to its ability as a racer, the quarter horse later proved an excellent worker with cattle. We would like to thank our friend, Nelson C. Nye, of Tucson, Arizona—*

the intention of establishing its capability in such an event, probably for purposes of comparison against those of the local and so far undefeated favourite, the men in the bushes felt certain their unauthorized spectating would be far from welcome. What was more, knowing who was involved, the owner of the livery barn had not needed the comment from Barnesley to alert him to the danger. The purchaser of the bay was not the sort of person upon whom it would be advisable, or safe, to be spying when he was engaged in an activity, the result of which he would prefer to keep to himself and his trusted helpers. Regardless of the fact that Staines in particular was not without prominence in the community of Grattan, being caught in the act would almost certainly result in painful repercussions.

At just over six foot, although two of his companions matched him in height and neither could be termed lightweights, Daniel Bernard "Bull" Keleney was by far the most bulky of the quartet under observation. When he wished to convey the impression, his florid features appeared expansively jovial and filled with bonhomie; a carefully cultivated luxuriant black moustache concealing the hard lines of his mouth. However, when angry, he had a habit of rolling his head from side to side, looking at everything and everybody from under his bushy eyebrows in the fashion of an old mossyhorn longhorn bull on the prod.

Owning controlling interests in many of the town's business concerns as well as a factory which supplied garments throughout Texas, had not given Keleney good taste in clothing. He had a pearl grey derby tilted at the back of a thinning thatch of hair which glistened even blacker from a liberal application of particularly pungent bay rum.[4] His three piece suit was made of excellent material and well cut, but his appearance was far from improved by it being a black and

---

one of the leading authorities on the breed, as well as being the author of numerous excellent action-escapism-adventure Western stories—for kindly supplying us with much useful information on the subject. J.T.E.

4 *"Bay rum:" an aromatic liquid, originally made by distilling rum with the leaves of the bayberry tree,* Pimenta racemosa, *but now consisting mainly of alcohol, water and essential oils. It was and still is used in medicines and cosmetics, but not intended for general beverage purposes. J.T.E.*

white check. Nor did the multi-hued silk cravat complement the lime green shirt. A bulky gold watch chain, from which dangled a trio of heavy seals, stretched across the front of his vest. His trousers were tucked untidily into low heeled riding boots. While he wore no weapons in plain view, it was common knowledge among the citizens of Gratton that he carried an ivory handled Colt Storekeeper Model Peacemaker[5] in a spring retention shoulder under the left side of his jacket and he had demonstrated his ability to use it when the need arose.

Accompanied by the burly hard-case who had helped him to remove the blanket, the small man who always rode Black Prince—Keleney's best and fastest quarter horse—led the bay gelding towards the two posts painted red and white, between which the races he organized were always started. Like Morris "Brick" Shatterhouse and Moses "Moe" Broody, although none of them had ever worked cattle on a ranch, Joseph "Little Joey" Cockburn was wearing cowhand style clothing. In keeping with their duties as enforcers of their employer's will, the larger pair had on gunbelts with Colt Peacemakers in the tied-down holsters. While the jockey had proved himself a competent gun and fist fighter, he was not armed at that moment.

Neither Keleney nor Shatterhouse followed the other two. Instead, they remained almost in front of the watchers' place of concealment. Drawing out the expensive Swiss-made watch attached to one end of the gold chain, the town boss glanced from it to the pair of blue and white posts he was facing. These were used to indicate the finishing line for the four hundred and forty yards' races. Holding the watch cupped in the palm of his massive right hand, he pressed the stud which caused the engraved lid of the "hunting case" to flip up and display the glass covered dial it protected. Then, as a further indication that he was getting ready to time the forthcoming trial, he swung his gaze to the other end of the course.

Receiving the final confirmation that Barnesley had been correct with regards to the quartet's purpose, Staines laid aside the field glasses and produced his own timepiece from his vest pocket. It was a somewhat battered looking B.W. Raymond

5 *For the benefit of new readers: details of the various types of the Colt Model P revolver, more generally known as the "Peacemaker," can be found in Footnote 21 of the* APPENDIX. *J.T.E.*

"railroad watch" made by the National Watch Company of Elgin, Illinois and had clearly seen a great deal of use. However, while it was not as elegant in appearance as the one held by Keleney, it possessed a similar "stop" mechanism and was noted for its accuracy throughout Dale County. Holding it ready for use, he too devoted his attention to the starting line.

Having passed the red and white posts, Cockburn turned the bay until it was facing in the direction from which it had come and was standing in the centre of the course. Raising his right foot, he placed it upon Broody's cupped hands and was given a boost on to the back of the gelding. That he required such assistance surprised none of the onlookers. They were aware that the necessity was caused by the specialized nature of the saddle upon which he settled himself with the deft ease acquired as a result of considerable training.

Experience gained over many years had taught men involved in the racing of horses over level ground and for comparatively short distances, that the more utilitarian styles of riding failed to produce the most satisfactory results when employed in such competitions.

Derived from the method of "hacking" brought by the colonists from Great—as it was *then*—Britain, using a "flat," single girthed rig, Eastern horsemen tended to sit in the middle of the saddle and not back on the cantle. With such a "seat," when the feet were properly placed, the stirrup leathers were straight up and down. Except in the case of a very tall rider on a small mount, the leathers were of such a length that—when sitting in the middle and allowing the legs to hang down as far as possible—the bottom of the stirrups and the ankle bones were level. A test of the correct length was for the rider to keep the feet level and stand erect in the saddle. If all was as it should be, in the majority of cases, there would be a clearance of about two inches between the rider and the rig.

Adequate as the revised version of the "English" seat had been found in the increasingly more developed and civilized East, where other means of transport were available for making longer journeys, it was soon found wanting by riders who needed to travel—or worked mainly on horseback—over the vast areas of open country west of the Mississippi River. Particularly where the cowhand was concerned, a different type of saddle and style of sitting upon it was found necessary.

Riding a horse which might not have acquired a full standard of training and which might frequently be called upon to perform extremely rapid manoeuvring at short notice when dealing with the longhorn cattle that were, at best, only half wild, the cowhand required greater security than offered by the "flat" Eastern rig.[6] With that in mind, drawing upon without adhering entirely to the type of saddles used by Mexican *vaqueros*, the fork and cantle were built up. Having acquired the habit of tying the end of the lariat to the horn when roping, as opposed to "dallying" it so it could be released hurriedly in an emergency, Texans also affixed a second girth to help withstand the strains which would be imposed.[7] As an aid to remaining on board when the mount was making rapid changes of direction, sliding halts, or even bucking, the Western rider—although retaining the same general length of the stirrup leathers used on the more effete "Eastern pleasure" rig—kept well back on the saddle.

Satisfactory as they were for the needs of their users, neither "Eastern" nor "Western" styles were suitable where a jockey in a "flat" race was concerned.

Having been helped to mount, Cockburn was perched upon the diminutive, feather-weight, single girthed saddle that was situated well up on the withers of the bay. He slipped the toes of his boots into the irons of the very short stirrups, already adjusted to his size, which were attached to the front of the front of the saddle. While the arrangement offered only a very precarious and far from comfortable seat, it had the inestimable advantage of placing all his weight in the most suitable position. Such a method of riding could not have been employed for any length of time, nor to cover a great distance. It was not intended to be, but was nevertheless ideal for its present purpose.

6 *Riders competing in polo games, or show jumping, etc., require different styles of saddles and "seats," but descriptions of these do not come within the province of this volume. J.T.E.*

7 *Although many Americans use the word "cinch" for the broad, short band made from coarsely woven horsehair, canvas or cordage which is terminated at each end with a metal ring which—together with the latigo—is used to fasten the saddle on a horse's back, because of its Spanish connotations, Texans employ the term "girth" and pronounce it as "girt." J.T.E.*

Controlling the gelding's eagerness to set off (its demeanour indicating that it knew what was expected of it and was willing to perform its function) Cockburn was watching Broody out of the corner of his eye. The hard-case was keeping their employer under observation and, receiving the prearranged signal that all was ready at the other end of the course, he raised his right hand with a grubby white handkerchief dangling from it.

"You ready, Joey?" Broody inquired.

"Ready!" the jockey confirmed, tensing slightly.

"Go!" the hard-case commanded in a shout, bringing down the handkerchief in a fluttering gesture.

Instantly, while two thumbs depressed knobs and set the "stop" mechanisms of their owners' respective watches into operation, Cockburn let out a yell and allowed the bay to lunge forward. Once it was in motion, the advantages offered by the so-called "monkey-seat" he was employing began to show.

As was attested by the outstretched nose and neck, the bay was straining every muscle and fibre of its powerful body to maintain the speed it built up from the moment it changed from moving restlessly on the spot to an almost immediate full gallop. Although the start was mainly achieved by the propulsive thrust of the puissant hind quarters, the motion threw most of its weight upon the front legs and they were almost transformed into its centre of balance.

If Cockburn had been sitting after the fashion of an Eastern or Western rider, he would have been a hindrance to his mount. Crouching on the diminutive saddle, with his torso inclined forward at the waist, he did more than just cut down the wind resistance offered by his body. Almost standing on the stirrups, the posture positioned all his weight directly over the withers and at his mount's centre of gravity. This ensured he created as little interference as possible with its balance and movements.

Urged onwards by the jockey, its hooves sinking slightly into the rain-softened surface of the course, the gelding sped in the direction of the finishing line. Glancing at it, the owner of the livery barn could see it was being induced to give of its best. What was more, it responded gallantly to the repeated summons it received. Then, as it passed between the blue and white posts, two thumbs tightened and the action of the "stop watch" mechanisms ceased to function.

"*Well?*" Barnesley hissed, exuding eagerness, as his companion stared at the face of the "railroad watch."

"Hot damn!" Staines ejaculated. "*Twenty-one* seconds!"

"Is that *good?*" the clerk inquired, although the tone employed by the owner of the livery barn was indicative that such was the case.

"*Good?*" Staines repeated, snapping his gaze to the other man's parched features. "I'll say it's *good*. That's faster than the Prince can do it by two seconds."

"Two seconds doesn't seem *much*," Barnesley protested.

"It's enough to get him over the finish line ahead of the Prince," Staines declared confidently, knowing the condition of the course was that most favoured by Keleney's very successful quarter horse. "And on soft going, too!"

"I don't follow you!" the clerk asserted.

"Some horses run better on hard ground, some when it's soft," Staines explained, trying to control his impatience. "The Prince always runs best when it's soft and so does that bay, only he does it better."

"Then it must be able to beat Mr. Keleney's horse?" Barnesley declared, more as a statement than a question.

"He can on a time like this," Staines agreed, tapping the face of his watch. Glancing to where Cockburn had brought the bay around and halted it in front of the town boss, he continued, "I'd give anything to hear what Bull and Little Joey're saying."

"I'm sure it would be most interesting," Barnesley admitted, but his voice had a timbre of nervousness. "However, it might not be wise to stay here any longer. They might decide to come and search in case somebody has been watching."

"They might at that," Staines conceded, less amused by the other's obvious perturbation than he might have been in different circumstances. He returned the watch to his vest-pocket. "Let's get going. There won't be anything clse for us to see."

CHAPTER TWO

Make Sure He Can't Blab

"Well," Daniel "Bull" Keleney said impatiently, his voice harsh and, despite having spent many years in the Southern States, still retaining the accent of one born on the already notorious East Side of New York. "Have they gone yet?"

"I can't see anything of 'em, boss," Brick Shatterhouse answered, having been scanning the bushes which had served as a point of vantage for Trader Staines and Ezekiel Barnesley. His mode of speech indicated his origins were closer to Kansas than Texas. Giving a shrug, he went on, "You told that miserable-looking quill-pusher to get the hell out of it as soon's they'd seen Three Socks here make his run and he *allus* does as you tell him."

"Likely," the town boss grunted. "But go up and make sure he has this time."

"Sure, boss," Shatterhouse assented.

"How was he, Joey?" Keleney inquired, as the hard-case set off up the slope to carry out the task.

"He's a better than fair mover, boss," Little Joey Cockburn claimed judiciously, having dismounted and patted the neck of the bay. He spoke with an accent similar to that of his employer. "But he's *not* another Black Prince."

"I wouldn't have let Staines see him run just now if I'd've

11

thought he might be," Keleney asserted looking upwards with a broad grin which displayed several gold teeth. Waiting until Shatterhouse emerged from the bushes, he let out a grunt of satisfaction as he received a wave indicating there were no other occupants. Then he addressed the second hard-case, "Start moving those posts back to where they should be, Moe. I don't want to be out here all day."

"Sure, boss," Moses Broody replied, sounding just a trace reluctant, but making the kind of response which he knew was always expected by his employer unless an answer in the negative was called for.

Although the trial was over, the owner of the livery barn had not been correct in his assumption that nothing of further interest would take place in the valley.

However, the work which the town boss had just ordered to be carried out was the part of his activities he would have objected to being observed by the onlookers.

Going to the nearer blue and white post, while Cockburn was attending to the bay gelding, Broody grasped and plucked it from the ground. Carrying it some yards along the course, he halted and pushed it into another hole. Never one to do any more work than was absolutely necessary, he contrived to take so long in ensuring it was seated properly that Shatterhouse had returned to the bottom of the valley and was moving the second post to its original position before he was finished.

"I'm ready, boss," Cockburn announced, having completed his work and replaced the quarter horse's blanket while the transferring of the posts was taking place. Knowing something of the purpose behind the "unsuspected" watching of the trial by Staines and Barnesley, he went on, "Do you reckon the Trader will spread the word about what's he's seen?"

"He'll let that bunch of son-of-bitches he goes around with know about it, if nobody else," Keleney answered confidently. "And, even if none of them pass on what he says, I've told Barnesley to make sure plenty of other folks hear how fast Socks can run. So the word'll get spread all right."

"And then they'll all start betting on him, figuring you aim to have him beat the Prince," the jockey continued, grinning in a knowing fashion. "You'll have taken them for plenty by the time they get to know different, boss."

"Can I help it if they figure it'll be *them* taking *me?*" the town boss asked, also grinning. "I just hope they'll have something left to bet with after tonight, though. Are you through, Brick, Moe?"

"Sure, boss," Shatterhouse confirmed, glancing at the holes from which the finishing posts had been removed. He and the other hard-case, having set up the posts, had just finished filling the cavities with the soil taken from them. "By tomorrow, there won't be nothing to show what we did; or that we've been here."

"Come on," Keleney ordered, after a quick look to satisfy himself that the claim made by Shatterhouse was correct. "Let's get Socks back to the cabin before anybody sees us with him."

Although the town boss shared the hard-case's confidence that there would be no trace of the subterfuge they had practiced the following day, neither of them thought to look in the direction of the starting line. If they had they would have noticed the grubby white handkerchief used by Broody to signal for the "trial" to commence. It had fallen from his pocket as he tried to put it away and lay just beyond the left side red and white post.

Shortly after Bull Keleney's party had taken their departure, Orville Webster, having arrived from Grattan by a roundabout route which caused him to miss being seen either by them or Trader Staines and Ezekiel Barnesley, came on to the rim above the valley. Noticing the marks left on the ground by the hooves of the bay, he descended the slope and walked towards them.

Tallish, fairly well built and in his late twenties, Webster was good looking in a studious fashion. For all that, he was tanned and moved with the easy grace of an athlete. As he was taking advantage of a public holiday to indulge in his hobby of studying natural history, he was wearing an open necked tartan shirt, Levi's pants and untanned walking boots instead of the more conventional attire in which he invariably dressed when teaching at the town's school.

Competent at his work, Webster had become popular with the children for whose education he was responsible. This was no mean feat for a young man holding such a position for the first time, especially when up against the kind of conditions which prevailed in Grattan. The ages of the boys and girls in the classes ranged from five to fourteen and they were not the most ruly of pupils, particularly some of the older ones. However, although he had succeeded in winning them over, there was something more sinister with which he had had to contend.

Bull Keleney had no wish for the younger generation of the town to acquire an education. The employees at his factory did not need to possess any great literacy to carry out their various tasks. Nor did he consider it desirable for them, or their potential successors, to attain it. Consequently, he was far from enthusiastic over the possibility of a generation growing up with a greater knowledge than their parents. Having that in mind, although he was too wise to openly contravene the rulings of the State Legislature with regards to the provision of scholastic facilities, he did all he could to reduce the effectiveness of the teacher's efforts. One of the chief arguments he put forward against the need to have an education was that, despite the fact that he had become very wealthy and was able to supply gainful employment for so many people in the town, he could neither read nor write.

Being by nature forceful and always determined to attain whatever he desired, the town boss had not restricted himself to merely dropping hints that an education was a needless encumbrance. Although he would have vehemently denied having given such instructions if questioned by the local law enforcement officers—an unlikely contingency, as they were all in his pay—knowing his sentiments, his hired hard-cases and members of the community wishing to curry favour made life as difficult and unpleasant as possible for the schoolteachers. Faced with considerable harassment from those factions and the general disinterest shown by the remainder of the population (or rather an almost unanimous disinclination to incur Keleney's wrath by showing support openly) a succession of schoolmistresses and masters of various ages and experience had come and gone over the years.

Latest and youngest incumbent to take the post, Webster had proved to be the most successful. Not only had he brought a new and less rigid outlook to the task, which enabled him to win the respect of the pupils, but he had also shown sufficient resilence of spirit to hold out against the apparent indifference

nd occasional open hostility shown by their elders. What was
more, having been a boxer of above average ability in college
who still kept himself physically fit, he had withstood
attempts at dissuading him from continuing his employment
by other than verbal means. In spite of having had an advantage in weight, Brick Shatterhouse was one who could testify
o the schoolteacher's fistic prowess and, accompanying his
attempts at exculpation with much profanity, occasionally did
o.

Surprising as it might have struck some of the people who
knew them only outside the classroom, one of the subjects in
which Webster had succeeded in interesting his pupils was art
appreciation. This had come about as a result of discovering
hat one of the older boys possessed considerable natural apti-
tude where producing drawings was concerned. An illustration
by the prodigy of horses galloping had provoked a vigorous
discussion, which the teacher had encouraged, when it was
displayed to the other members of the class.

As was the usual and generally accepted practice, the artist
had portrayed the animals running with the fore- and hind-legs
extended simultaneously ahead and behind. Another pupil had
protested that he did not believe any horse could attain such a
posture even at a gallop. The artist had agreed, but claimed he
had never seen a picture which differed from his conception.
When nobody else had been able to suggest what actually took
place under such circumstances, the pupils had turned to their
teacher for adjudication as had become their habit. Admitting
he was no better informed on the matter, although he too had
always had doubts about the accuracy of the paintings, he had
promised to find the answer for them before school commenced after the holiday.

Having failed to obtain the requisite information from any
of the small circle of friends he had made among the men of
the town, even the owner of the livery barn having professed
ignorance where the matter was concerned, Webster had been
reconciled to being compelled to announce he was unable to
supply the information to his pupils. However, his arrival at
the valley had had nothing to do with his dilemma. Taking a
constitutional walk, combined with continuing his studies of
the wild animals and plant life in the area, nothing more than
chance had brought him in that direction.

Webster had known nothing about the supposed trial of a quarter horse, although his suspicions might have been aroused if he had been aware of who had carried it out. On coming into view, his scrutiny of the course along which i had been run led him to consider that a closer examination might be worthwhile and prove informative. His decision was not provoked by any desire to discover what had taken place as such. Due to the heavy rain the previous night all signs of the earlier races had washed away, and the ground was ideally suited to exhibiting the traces left by the latest users. As only one horse was involved, and as he had acquired a sound knowledge of reading tracks prior to coming to Grattan, studying the marks produced by the horse's hooves as it ran along the otherwise unscarred centre of the course might allow him to solve his problem.

The young schoolteacher had, therefore, no ulterior motive; just a desire to avoid letting down his pupils.

Crossing to where the hoof marks indicated the change from a comparatively motionless stand to running at the starting line, Webster advanced slowly along the course and studied them as he went. He had occasionally thought of the way in which artists tended to create the impression of horses in rapid motion and, subconsciously, tried to verify or discredit the posture. Now he was presented with a motive and the opportunity to investigate the matter. Such was the skill he had acquired at reading tracks, that he found himself able to form an estimation of what had taken place as the animal had sped along the course towards the finishing line.

Wishing to gain corroboration for his suppositions, the schoolteacher retraced his footsteps when he reached the two blue and white posts and repeated the examination. On arriving at the finishing line for the second time, he was satisfied that he had attained the required solution.

The artists were wrong!

At no time when galloping had the horse had all four hooves off the ground at the same moment!

Instead, the gait was for one hind foot to impact upon the ground. Then the front foot of the same side descended simultaneously with the other hind foot. Finally, the remaining hoof—known to horsemen as the "leading foot," although Webster was unaware of the term—came down and the sequence was repeated.

Despite having passed them twice, being engrossed in his examination of the tracks to the exclusion of all else, the schoolteacher did not notice the still discernible marks left by the finishing posts when they had been moved nearer to the starting line and then returned to their original positions.

Even more important, Webster paid no attention to the grubby white handkerchief lying where it had been dropped by its owner!

Unfortunately, unbeknown to the schoolteacher, the latter part of his activities were being observed and their purpose misunderstood!

"Did you find the god-damned wipe?" Bull Keleney demanded, he and his other two men having halted on seeing Moses Broody approaching at a gallop.

"No, boss," the hard-case admitted, bringing his mount to a stop. He went on hurriedly as a scowl came to his employer's face. "'Least-wise I didn't go and pick it up—!"

"Then why the 'something'[1] hell didn't you?" the town boss challenged, before the explanation could be completed.

"That 'mother-something' schoolteacher was down in the valley when I got there," Broody replied. "He was going along it like he was reading sign."

The hard-case had not discovered the loss of his handkerchief until he and his companions had covered about a mile. On being told it was missing, Keleney had ordered him to go and find it. Guessing where he had dropped it, he had returned to the valley. However, on seeing Orville Webster when he reached the top of the slope, he had halted so as to be able to continue watching undetected. Drawing a partly erroneous conclusion with regards to the schoolteacher's activities, he had decided to ignore his employer's instructions and hurry after the rest of the party to warn them of his suppositions.

"So what?" Brick Shatterhouse scoffed, wishing to belittle the young man who had beaten him in the fist fight they had had. "He doesn't know sic 'em about doing it."

"The hell he doesn't!" Keleney contradicted, being better informed about Webster's ability at reading tracks. "From what I've heard tell, he knows enough to be able to figure out what we've been up to."

1 *See*: Author's Note, Paragraph Two. *J.T.E.*

"Even if *he* doesn't," Little Joey Cockburn supplemented. "Should he tell the Trader, or Sam Williams, *they'd* soon enough figure it out. And, once they did, they'd make sure everybody else got to know as well. Which'd spoil everything for you, boss."

"It would!" Keleney conceded grimly.

Because of the repeated successes attained by the Black Prince, the town boss had noticed there was a growing reluctance to wager upon the races in which it participated. Or rather to wager in a way not beneficial to him, via the professional gamblers he employed to attend the contests and act as "bookmakers." Even though it was being run at increasingly high "odds on," meaning the bettors had to stake a larger sum than they would receive in return on winning, most of the money had been placed on it.

Relying upon the betting at the races and gambling upon other "sporting" events he organized to retrieve a fair proportion of the money he paid to his employees, even to the extent of keeping some of them so deeply in debt they were virtually his slaves, Keleney had considered such a state of affairs most undesirable. Never one to be troubled by scruples, he had decided to put the unsatisfactory conditions to rights. He was not too proud to seek expert advice and had consulted with Cockburn upon how he might best achieve his purpose. Considering the various schemes put forward by the jockey, whose exposed dishonesty had caused him to quit the more lucrative race courses of the East and ride under an assumed named in Texas, the town boss had selected and elaborated upon the one he felt most suited to his needs.

The fake trial had been arranged to encourage betting which would be more favourable to Keleney's interests, as Cockburn had assumed, but it also had a second purpose that was unknown to any of the men who he had selected to be his assistants.

Despite Keleney having contrived to own the majority of the businesses in and around the town, either openly or indirectly, there were still a few which remained free from his control. Their owners, Trader Staines and the owner of the post office—who also acted as local agent for the Overland Stage Company—Samuel Williams, being two, they were all beyond his reach for one reason or another. Although they had

o far been too cautious to display open hostility, or opposition
o his wishes, he was aware that collectively they posed a
potential threat to his domination. This continued to be latent
rather than active, but he was not enamoured of its existence.
As long as they remained in Grattan, they prevented him from
being able to achieve his ambition of exerting unchallenged
influence throughout the whole of Dale County.

Accepting that to cause the removal of all the dissidents
forcibly would be impolitic, Keleney was always on the look-
out for ways by which their standing in the community might
be lessened. He had seen how, in addition to producing a
profitable outcome from the quarter horse race which was part
of the holiday entertainments he had arranged, he might help
bring this about. It was unlikely that Staines would keep the
apparent result of the "secret trial" to himself. Even if he did,
Ezekiel Barnesley was under orders to make sure the news of
it was circulated and to cause credit for this to be given to the
owner of the livery barn. Pressed for further details, as was
certain to happen, Staines would have to tell what he had seen
and deduced. His reputation as one who knew a great deal
about horses would ensure his summations were given credence and acted upon.

However, good as the bay gelding looked, it could not
match the performance of the Black Prince. Its seemingly very
fast pace had only come about because Staines had relied upon
the positions of the finishing posts to establish the time it had
taken to cover the distance. Having run for less than the four
hundred and forty yards, Three Socks gave the impression of
having done so far more swiftly than the best speed ever
attained by the town boss's favourite over the full distance.
Consequently, when the event took place, those who acted
upon Staines advice—and Keleney was confident many of the
population would—were going to lose their money. As a
result of this, they and everybody else who heard what happened, would be less likely to listen to their informant and his
associates in the future.

Until hearing of Webster's presence and actions on the race
course, the town boss had been sure his scheme was progress-
ing exactly as he required. Barnesley had brought Staines to
the bushes at the top of the valley and the "trial" had been
med with the required conclusions being drawn. The finish-

ing posts had been returned to their original positions, but some indications of their removal and re-positioning were unavoidable. These would have been less noticeable the following day and Keleney would have some of his men placed to hide them.

However, the intervention of the schoolteacher seemed to be putting the entire scheme in jeopardy!

Such was the devious way in which Keleney's mind worked, he did not take into consideration the possibility that Webster's presence in the valley was no more than chance. He believed that somehow—despite the instructions given to Barnesley—having the suspicious mind of a horse-trader, Staines had suspected a trick and enlisted help to double check what happened without the clerk becoming aware of his intentions. In which case, the schoolteacher was sufficiently intelligent to make the correct deductions from what he saw.

There was more than just the loss of the anticipated revenue from the misdirected betting to be taken into account if the scheme was exposed.

So efficiently had all Keleney's other gambling coups been organized that his involvement was never established. In fact, he had always been careful to give the impression that he too was a loser—and on a larger scale than anybody else—when an "unexpected" turn of events caused the apparently certain result of the wagers to be reversed. While the dissidents in particular might have had their suspicions, so far they had been unable to obtain confirmation.

The discoveries which the town boss believed Webster had made could supply the required proof!

Keleney had never been a man to stand idly by and allow a situation which might threaten him to continue unchecked!

"Brick!" the town boss said. "You and Moe go find the schoolteacher. Make sure he can't blab about what he's seen."

"You mean make sure *permanent*, boss?" Shatterhouse inquired hopefully.

"That's just what I mean," Keleney confirmed, thinking of the way in which the schoolteacher was improving the education of the children. "Only make sure it looks like it happened in an accident—Or he was killed by somebody when they were robbing him."

CHAPTER THREE

Four to One on the Local Gal

Letting himself into the main classroom of the school, Orville Webster frowned. Although he had closed and locked the door of his living quarters at the rear when he went out, he saw it was now standing slightly ajar. What was more, despite the front of the building being in darkness, someone had lit the lamp in the dining-room section while he was absent. Deciding that the woman who did his cleaning and cooking must have paid a visit during his absence, he strolled along the aisle between the desks of the pupils. Crossing the open space at the front of the classroom, passing his own raised desk and blackboard, he went unconcernedly towards the door.

Although the schoolteacher was unaware of the fact, he was already living on borrowed time!

With his examination of the tracks left by Bull Keleney's bay gelding conducted satisfactorily, as far as he was concerned, and having no idea that his studies had incurred the wrath of the town boss, Webster had set off to continue his studies of the local flora and fauna. Finding nothing of interest in the vicinity of the valley, he had walked across the rolling range country at a lively pace as he searched for something to which he considered it would be worth-while devoting his attention. He had moved so quickly, he was out of sight before Brick Shatterhouse and Moe Broody arrived at the scene of the fake trial.

Regardless of the way in which each was dressed, the two hard-cases were not outdoors' men and they possessed few of the skills acquired by those who worked regularly on the open range country. On reaching the valley and finding their quarry had already vacated it, being aware of their limitations in that field, they made no attempt to seek out his tracks as an aid to locating him. Instead, deducing incorrectly that he would be returning to Grattan to pass on the information he had collected, they had set off with the intention of catching him before he arrived. Having failed to come across him as they rode along, due—although they did not know it—to their erroneous conclusions, they had ascertained that he had not eluded them somehow and reached the town. Satisfied on that point, they had selected a building which allowed them to keep watch for his return by the most probable route and waited for him to come back.

Pure chance had prevented Webster from being waylaid by Shatterhouse and Broody as he was approaching the town!

The schoolteacher was fortunate in that he had come across various animals and birds which interested him, and he had travelled further and spent longer than was his original intention. What was more, his ramblings had caused him to travel in almost a half circle around the town. Furthermore, he had become so engrossed in his studies, it was not until the sun had almost reached the western horizon that he became conscious of how much time had elapsed. Nor had he appreciated just how much distance he had covered. Although his sense of direction was sufficient to prevent him from getting lost, because darkness descended before he had gone far, his return took longer than would have been the case if he had been walking in daylight.

When he reached Grattan, despite knowing that he was going to be late in joining those of the local men with whom he was on terms of close acquaintance at the Bull's head Saloon, Webster did not go there immediately. Always conscious of appearances, he had no desire to be seen in a public place wearing such old and now, as a result of his activities during the day, grubby clothing. With that in mind, he had circled around the outskirts of the town and reached the schoolhouse without passing through the streets. He had therefore avoided the men positioned to prevent him reaching the homes of his associates or joining them in the saloon.

As soon as he pushed open the door of the living quarters, the schoolteacher became aware that he was in error with his summations!

Every drawer of the sidepiece was open, with some of the contents dangling out or lying on the floor. The four silver cups Webster had won in college for his athletic prowess were missing from its top. Nor was this the only evidence that something was radically wrong. Judging from what he could see where he was standing, the rest of the room had been just as thoroughly ransacked.

Nothing within the schoolteacher's range of vision suggested Mrs. Rafferty had been the visitor in his absence. Even if she had come for some reason and decided to light the lamp for him in case he returned after nightfall, it was inconceivable that she would have left his quarters in such a state of disarray.

Therefore, somebody else must be responsible!

Even as the appreciation of the situation came and Webster was on the point of going to summon official assistance, small though his faith in the abilities of the town marshal might be, he heard a scuffling sound from the bedroom. Its door was half open and it too was illuminated by its lamp. Although the perpetrator was hidden from his view, hearing the crash of glass and seeing the shattered photograph of his parents thrown from the dressing-table to the floor, he grew too angry to put his sensible intentions into operation.

Driven by an emotion of fury too powerful to be resisted, the schoolteacher lunged forward. As he crossed the threshold, in spite of his attention being focussed upon the partially open door of the bedroom, a sensation of movement to the left caught the corner of his eye. Instinct rather than conscious thought caused him to turn his head in that direction. The sight which met his eyes was so fraught with menace, it set an alarm ringing through his brain.

Holding a hunting knife raised with the clip pointed blade

extended below the heel of the hand,[1] so as to be able to deliver a powerful downwards chop to the side of the neck, a big and burly masculine figure was coming from where he had been hiding concealed by the wall. In spite of the bandana which masked most of the would-be attacker's face and the mode of attack being that generally employed by Indians, his build and attire allowed Webster to identify him.

It was Brick Shatterhouse!

Never one to allow a project he had set into motion to be given up because it had met with a set-back, Keleney had refused to be deterred by the news of the schoolteacher's failure to return before sundown. He had ordered a watch to be kept on those places to which Webster was likely to deliver the news about the fake trial. The men assigned to the task were under orders to stop their quarry without noise or in any other way arousing attention and, if successful, they were to take his body to the schoolhouse. As a precaution, in case he went there before visiting his associates and to make everything ready for his arrival if he should be intercepted elsewhere, Shatterhouse and Moses Broody were sent to create the impression that a robbery had taken place and to await his coming one way or the other.

The two hard-cases had completed their primary task before Webster arrived. On hearing him enter, they had had sufficient respect for his ability as a fighter to lay the trap into which he had walked!

Shatterhouse had borrowed the knife in the dual hope that he might be presented with an opportunity to avenge the thrashing he had received at the hands of the schoolteacher, and to do so in a way which would suggest the killing was done by a robber caught on the premises. In spite of his presence having been detected before he could complete his attack, he did not consider there was any undue cause for concern. As he had surmised would happen when making his plan, while he was lying in wait alongside the door, Broody

---

1 *"Clip point:" where, as is the case on all traditional "bowie" knives, the last few inches of the otherwise unsharpened back of the blade joins and becomes an extension of the cutting edge in a concave arc. A "spear" point is formed by both sides coming together in symmetrical curves. J.T.E.*

had been in the bedroom and had created the diversion which brought their intended victim across the threshold in a less cautious fashion than might have been the case if he had been caught unawares.

Regardless of the hard-case's suppositions, the school-teacher did not prove to be the helpless dupe he envisaged.

Recognizing the intended assailant merely served as an added stimulus which set Webster's defensive reflexes into motion. Without consciously considering what to do for the best, he spun swiftly to his left. While he was still turning, he clenched his right fist and, taking a step forward instead of retreating as might have been expected, he shot it out. Before the knife could commence its descent, his knuckles smashed into the centre of the masked face though the punch was, of necessity, hurriedly thrown, it was propelled by all the strength and skill he could muster. Nor did he need to feel disappointed at the result it achieved.

As he was taken unawares by the unexpected nature and rapidity of the schoolteacher's response, the effect of the blow upon Shatterhouse was particularly potent. Feeling as if it had suddenly erupted into flames, his head snapped backwards. Letting the knife fall from his grasp, his hands rose instinctively to the stricken area and he reeled away from his intended victim. Dazed and more than half blinded by the tears which were involuntarily filling his eyes, he was in no condition to defend himself from a continuation of the attack. Nor did the idea of alerting his companion to the drastically changed state of affairs occur to him.

The need for defense did not arise!

No attack was delivered!

While brave, Webster was neither reckless nor foolhardy!

The fact that Shatterhouse was wearing a mask and the way in which he had acted gave unmistakable warning of his intentions. These were not merely to commit a robbery. What was more, the sounds and activity from inside the bedroom were proof that he had at least one accomplice close by.

Being unarmed as usual, but feeling certain the same would not apply to whoever had broken and thrown down the photograph of his parents, the schoolteacher wisely concluded that discretion was the better part of valour. Without waiting to discover whether his suppositions were correct, or how many more men he would be in contention with if he remained, he spun around and darted out through the door into the classroom. His only hope for survival, he realized, was to flee to the home of one of his small group of friends. Once he was outside the building and in the darkness, he felt sure he could achieve his purpose.

Unfortunately, Webster's luck was at last running out!

Having been interested in finding out whether his companion's scheme was working, Broody had come to the door of the bedroom to watch. He arrived an instant after things started to go wrong.

Realizing that it was up to him to rectify the situation, the hard-case sprang forward. Paying no attention to Shatterhouse as he ran across the sitting-room, he did not attempt to draw his revolver. Nor was there any need for him to do so. He had kept with him the new Winchester Model of 1873 rifle with which he had intended to kill Webster from a distance if presented with an opportunity on the range or while approaching the town. He had been holding it when creating the disturbance and it was still in his grasp.

One glance as he went through the door into the classroom warned Broody that he could not catch up with and tackle the fleeing schoolteacher quickly enough to prevent an escape from the building. Nor, having seen what happened to his companion, was he willing to try. Neither was there any need, if it came to the point. Their orders were not to take Webster alive, but to kill him. There was another, much safer way of doing this than with bare hands.

Skidding to a halt, the hard-case threw the lever of the Winchester through its loading cycle and snapped the butt to his right shoulder. Bracing himself, he sighted along the thirty inch octagonal barrel rather than using the sights. Mentally blessing the mistrust which had caused him to keep the weapon with him instead of leaving it in the backroom of the Bull's Head Saloon, he squeezed the trigger when satisfied with his aim. The hammer lashed forward, setting the process of detonation into motion and causing a flat-nosed .44 calibre bullet to be discharged. Flying true, it struck Webster in the centre of the back.

Watching through the smoke of the ignited black powder, Broody saw the schoolteacher reel under the impact. Propelled by forty grains of powder, which created a muzzle energy of seven hundred and fifty-two foot-pounds and a velocity of thirteen hundred feet per second, the two hundred grains of lead shattered his spine. His brief onwards progress was as involuntary as that of a chicken starting to run after its head had been chopped off. Crumpling forward as the impetus died and reflexes ceased to function, he struck and shoved the door of the building to a close.

Once again operating the lever, but paying no attention to the empty cartridge case which was ejected to make way for the next live round from the tubular magazine, Broody was moving forward by the time his victim fell. He was not entirely at ease over having had to use the Winchester, but reassured himself with the thought that there had been no other choice. Once the schoolteacher had left the building, even if he did not start shouting to raise the alarm, any shooting would almost certainly have attracted unwanted attention. As it was, having been done within the confines of the walls, there was less danger of the detonation from the rifle's charge of black powder being overheard.

Throwing a quick look at Webster in passing and concluding, from the untidily abandoned way in which he was lying that he was dead, Broody opened the door a little and peered cautiously outside. Only the usual early evening sounds of the town came to his ears. There were neither shouted questions, nor any other indications, that the shot had been heard and inquisitive citizens were coming to investigate.

Waiting for a few seconds to satisfy himself that all was well, the hard-case withdrew his head and closed the door. Being eager to go to the saloon and watch the entertainment which was to take place that evening, he was in no mood to waste any more time. Without so much as another glance at the young man whose life he had brought to an end, he rested the barrel of the Winchester on his right shoulder and strode swiftly towards the sitting-room to tell Shatterhouse, who he could hear savagely blaspheming, that he had carried out the most important part of the instructions given by their employer.

"Four to one on the local gal to win. Come on, you sporting gentlemen. I've got all this money and I'm willing to put it where my mouth is. Come on, I say. Who wants it? If you don't speculate, you'll never accumulate. I'll give anybody who wants it four to one up to any sum you name to cover that Maggie Bollinger beats Countess Tanya."

The speaker, whose words were attracting considerable attention in his immediate vicinity, was wearing attire which indicated he was a prosperous and successful professional gambler. Therefore, the ability to make an assessment of chances was a most important part of his trade and much of his livelihood depended upon him drawing the correct conclusions. Under different circumstances, or if they had been less engrossed in what was taking place, his audience might have found his declaration puzzling. Certainly it seemed he was being extremely rash in offering to risk even a portion of the money he was exhibiting so flambouyantly upon such a dubious proposition. The "local gal" had a slight advantage in weight, was somewhat younger and had put up a creditable performance in the early stages of the "new style" wrestling bout.[1] However, this was no longer the case. Everything was now suggesting that the superior skill of her opponent was making it extremely unlikely she would justify his confidence by attaining the requisite victory.

Clearly, if the way in which those about him began to accept the wager was any guide, there were many present who considered the gambler's offer ill-advised and wished to take full advantage of his remarkably poor judgement.

Strange as it might seem, on each side of the raised square dais at the centre of the crowded barroom in the Bull's Head Saloon, there was at least one man who appeared to possess a similarly misguided faith in the ability of the "local gal" to win. Nor were any of them finding a lack of spectators, including Daniel "Bull" Keleney, who were equally willing to make the most of the opportunity which was being presented by their apparent lack of judgement.

While civic pride would have caused the local members of the audience to hope Maggie Bollinger would defeat the stranger to the town (and they would have been delighted to

1 *We realize that the fate of Orville Webster and the nature of the contest recorded in this Chapter differ from those which were given in:* Part One, Dusty Fog in "The Schoolteacher," THE HARD RIDERS. *This is because we have been supplied with the correct facts—which were not available to us when we produced the book in 1962—by Dusty's grandson, for whom we also have the honour of being official biographer. See the various volumes of the* Alvin Dustine "Cap" Fog *series. J.T.E.*

see it happen) appearances now suggested this was unlikely to happen and it seemed a pity to miss the chance to make some easy money.

No matter whether a male spectator was betting or not, he would have been hard to please if he was not enjoying the latest form of entertainment being put on by Keleney. Even the girls employed in the saloon were enjoying it, and not a few of them were wagering on the result. However, the pleasure being derived by the majority of the men in the audience was not solely dependent upon the opportunity to gamble while watching a bout of wrestling under new and much more exciting rules than was usually the case. Neither contestant could be described as exceptionally beautiful, but they were far from ugly. What was more, the way in which each was clad added to the attraction for the men who were watching them.

Close to five foot ten inches in height, Maggie Bollinger was shapely in a buxom fashion. Normally cheerful, her good looking features showed exhaustion and not a little suffering as she was once more dragging herself laboriously erect after having been thrown to the reasonably well padded floor of the ring. Her exertions had caused her shortish black hair to resemble a sodden woollen mop. Soaked with perspiration, the now dirty white masculine undershirt and cheap black dancer's tights, the latter being laddered and kneeless, clung to her well endowed body like a second skin. As these were her sole raiment, they gave indisputable proof that there was no flabby fat to mar her eye-catching curves. Rather she was muscled in a way to be expected of one who frequently helped her husband to carry out his work as the local blacksmith.

An inch shorter, at forty-three years of age, "Countess" Tanya Bulganin—the claim to nobility being no more than a figment of her manager's imagination—was ten years older than her opponent. Despite being about six pounds lighter, she was almost as well developed. Her blonde hair was equally dishevelled and she was showing that she too had been subjected to considerable strenuous physical effort. However, there was now a broad grin on her sallow and sullen, yet faintly attractive, Slavic face. She too wore black tights, of better quality although just as badly damaged in the lengthy conflict. Above them, leaving her midriff bare, was a sleeveless white satin bodice the decollete of which was daring in the extreme.

Even when dry, which it was not at the moment, the latter garment left nobody in doubt that it alone covered her massive bosom. In spite of her bulk, like her opponent, she had proved surprisingly agile and was just as well muscled.

Although satisfied that victory was inevitable, Tanya had no intention of bringing an immediate end to the bout. In addition to remembering the instructions she had received from her manager, she had another reason for wanting it to continue. The local woman she had originally expected would have been easy meat, as was generally the case in the towns they visited unless she found herself opposed by another professional female wrestler. But this opponent had proved much more competent and far tougher than she had anticipated. What was more, as a result of having been over confident in the opening minutes of the bout, she had found herself taking the worst of the struggle and, for once without having allowed it to happen of her own accord, she was pinned to lose the first fall.

Having pride in her ability, but being deficient in sporting spirit, the blonde had not been enamoured of losing. Nor had she been made any more amiable by the difficulty she had had in taking the equalizing fall. She had required all her strength and skill, aided by a few illegal moves unnoticed by the referee to gain the victory. Now, with her superior ability having granted her the upper hand, she meant to make the other woman suffer for as long as possible before causing the end of the bout.

Advancing on Maggie, who was swaying on spread apart feet while adopting a protective stance, Tanya caught her by the right wrist and swung her around. Propelled backwards against the hard turnbuckle in a corner of the ring, she bounced from it. Stepping aside as she was driven forwards, the blonde drove linked hands between her shoulder blades and sent her in a helpless plunge on to her hands and knees near the opposite corner. Grinning broadly, Tanya strolled to where her manager was standing on the apron beyond the ropes. Accepting the schooner of beer he offered, she drank deeply and watched the local man who was acting as referee begin the count which might establish her fallen opponent was beaten. She hoped the other would rise so she could continue the punishment.

CHAPTER FOUR

It's Over and She's Beaten

Looking around the bar-room of the Bull's Head Saloon as he was making his way towards his seat at the side of the ring, after having made a sizeable wager on "Countess" Tanya Bulganin beating Maggie Bollinger in the wrestling bout, Daniel "Bull" Keleney felt satisfied with almost everything he saw.

All in all, the town boss considered that his affairs were going smoothly and pretty much as he wanted.

Not only had Orville Webster been prevented from warning his associates that the trial of the quarter horse was a fake, but the prevention had been carried out in a way which—Keleney now realized—would be far less likely to arouse suspicion, or speculation as to the motive, than if his death had taken place on the range or while he was approaching the town. Furthermore, his murder—the news of which had not yet been made public—would cause a considerable disruption to the education of the children. It would be difficult to replace him with somebody for whom they would feel the kind of respect he had engendered and which made them apply themselves so willingly to their studies. Whoever came to take his place, and—with the reputation that the school had and with the apparent antipathy of the citizens of Grattan where teachers were concerned—it was unlikely there would be many appli-

31

cants, was going to find the pupils a restless and disturbed bunch, unwilling to settle down to their interrupted lessons.

With luck, aided by the usual kind of treatment from the hard-cases and those local citizens wishing to curry favour, the replacement would fail to establish the kind of rapport that Webster had attained. In which case, the disgruntled new schoolteacher could be induced by less violent means to go elsewhere. While Keleney had no qualms over employing violence if other means failed, he realized that to do so under the present circumstances might be unwise. Coming so soon after the murder of the previous incumbent, it might cause pressure for an investigation by the Texas Rangers. They would perform the task with far greater diligence than the Town Marshal Hawley Grenville; who already knew of the murder, but was carrying out the instructions he had been given over how it should be handled.

As the threat of exposure was now removed, the proposed betting coup on the forthcoming quarter horse race was showing signs of yielding the desired result. Although the owner of the livery barn had not been talkative of his own accord, either because he was waiting to hear from the schoolteacher or because he meant to keep his information for the benefit of himself and his immediate circle of cronies, Ezekiel Barnesley had caused the story of the "trial" and its "result" to be spread. Regardless of whether Staines had been consulted and told what he had or had not seen, there had been sufficient indications for Keleney to feel sure the "unexpected" arrival of Three Socks would produce the required effect. Among other things, the gamblers who regularly acted as "bookmakers" had informed him they were already being asked what odds they would be offering against the Black Prince if he failed to win.

Aided by the way in which Keleney had been acting, even before Brick Shatterhouse and Moses Broody delivered the news of how they had disposed of the schoolteacher, with the latter insisting upon claiming the majority of the credit, the evening's activities were going as well as he had anticipated. Primed by the two free drinks each had received on arrival, the customers were clearly enjoying the unusual spectacle presented by the wrestling bout between two well endowed and, for that day and age, extremely scantily dressed women. There was an added fillip because one of the combatants was known to practically everybody in the bar-room. Furthermore, the bonus he had paid to his entire work force was inducing even those recipients who were not gambling on the contest to be in the mood to celebrate and spend more of the extra money they had received than they might have otherwise intended.

As was always the case in such circumstances, the behaviour of the town boss had helped to create the desired mood among his employees. Moving among the crowd before the commencement of the bout, there had been not the slightest hint that he had ordered the death of another human being and was waiting to be told it had been done. Instead, he had been bonhomie personified. Slapping a man on the shoulder in passing, bellowing with laughter at even the most feeble of jokes he was told and coming back with one far better, he had given the kind of impression long experience had taught him would best serve his purpose.

At such times, the men who toiled for the enrichment of Keleney forgot their long hours of labour and the poor conditions under which they worked. While he might not pay as well as did other factories of a similar kind, few of them gave a cash bonus every couple of months or so or arranged so many forms of diverting and enjoyable entertainment. Also, in their opinion, not many other bosses would walk among and joke with their employees; but "Bull" was never too full of his success to do so. As a result, they regarded him as a prince of good fellows and considered it a privilege to be in his employ.

"Aren't you betting, Sam, Trader?" the town boss inquired, coming to a stop by two men whom he felt sure did not share the opinion of his employees where he was concerned.

"Nope," Sam Williams replied and his companion also signified a negative response. "I'm not betting."

Tall, lean and leathery, with a pleasant face, the speaker was well dressed. Yet he looked far from comfortable in the collar and necktie which was not generally a part of his attire. While there was no discernible animosity in his drawling Texan's voice, neither did it have the timbre of friendship and respect which was shown to the town boss by others in the room.

Before any more could be said, Maggie was hauling herself from the canvas with the aid of the ropes and the referee had stopped counting. Handing the beer schooner she had emptied to her small, flashily dressed and sharp featured manager, Tanya strode swiftly across the ring. Sinking both hands into the bosom of the local woman and eliciting a sharp gasp of pain, she pulled forward and pushed. On being released, Maggie was sent against the ropes. Their springiness threw her forward. Once again, the blonde stepped aside. This time, however, she swung around her leg so its knee rammed into her opponent's stomach. Letting out a croaking gasp, Maggie folded at the middle and collapsed.

"Looks like that four to one's a right foolish bet," Keleney remarked, but there was just a trace of a suggestion that he was not as enamoured of the prospect of winning as might have been expected.

"*Real* foolish, way things *look*," Williams conceded in tones which were mildly sardonic. "I'd've thought those gamblers of your'n had better sense than that, Bull."

"*My* gamblers, Sam?" the town boss queried, as if surprised by the suggestion, watching the referee remonstrating with Tanya for having grabbed Maggie by the bosom instead of commencing to count. "None of *my* gamblers would be that stupid, or they wouldn't stay *my* gamblers for long."

"You letting *outsiders* take bets now, Bull?" Staines inquired.

"Why not?" Keleney countered and, to men who knew him as well as the pair he was addressing, there was an indication of asperity in his seemingly amiable reply. "They came here when they heard the Countess was wrestling and asked could they make bets. Seeing as they were willing to let me have a rake-off on their take, what had I to lose by saying 'yes'?"

"Nary a thing," Williams admitted, with such sincerity that he might have believed what he was told.

"I thought you boys would want to get in on it, way things stand," Keleney went on, nodding to where the referee was about to start counting. "Winning at those odds would be like finding money in the street."

"Might at that," the owner of the post office drawled. "Only my daddy always told me never to call no bet that looked like it wasn't going to pay off for the gambling man's made it. Allowed such was a fool bet and like' to cost you money no matter how much things looked's if you'd be sure to win."

"A smart man, your old daddy," the town boss asserted, but his smile did not reach his eyes.

"*Real* smart," Williams confirmed. "Many's the time folks allowed's how he should've took on as a schoolteacher."

Drawing an erroneous conclusion, as he did not realize that the comment had been intended as nothing more than a facetious dig at his much vaunted lack of education and illiteracy, Keleney tensed and stared hard at the postmaster. He was unable to detect anything from the impassive leathery features. Nor was he any more successful in the attempt at reading emotions when he glanced at Staines.

The town boss found the complete lack of reaction puzzling. Not that, knowing the respective abilities of the two men as poker players, had he expected to see much. Nor had he believed either would have bet, even upon such an apparently sure thing as the result of the wrestling bout, knowing he was the organizer. He had, in fact, started the conversation in the hope of picking up a hint of their feelings with regards to the quarter horse race which was to take place the following afternoon and had considered, skilled as they were in controlling their feelings, that he ought to be able to detect a hint if they were suspicious. From his scrutiny, he concluded this was not the case. However, the deduction did nothing to clarify the situation. They should have been worried because the schoolteacher had not put in an appearance, but both seemed relaxed and at ease.

The sight of what was taking place in the ring diverted Keleney's attention from the problem.

Although part of her wanted to remain on the mat, Maggie had too much spirit to yield to the suggestion. Instead, having been granted a badly needed respite by the referee delaying the count while remonstrating with Tanya, she was able to rise before it was completed. Watching the other woman standing up, the blonde was delighted by the prospect of being able to inflict more suffering. However, as she was about to advance and continue the attack, she swayed and felt a momentary sensation of dizziness. Shaking her head to clear it she moved confidently forward.

Bringing up her hands as she saw her opponent coming towards her, Maggie was too close to exhaustion to react with her former speed. Once again, before she could come to grips, she felt her breasts grabbed. The fingers and thumbs gouged savagely into the sensitive mounds and their scanty covering offered no protection. So excruciating was the pain which assailed her, that it numbed her brain and prevented her from doing anything effective, even if it was only grasping Tanya's wrists in an attempt to pull the hands from their grip.

Paying no attention to the protests of the referee, the blonde ran her all but helpless opponent backwards across the ring and into the ropes. Using their spring to give an added impulsion, she was surprised to feel herself weakening as she swivelled and flung Maggie in the opposite direction. However, although the spasm lasted slightly longer than the one she had experienced just before commencing the attack, it too died away and she felt ready to continue.

Going across the ring in a twirling rush which she was unable to control, the local contender was facing the centre when she reached the other side. For all that, her position was not quite as desperate as it appeared to the spectators. The pain she had suffered from the claw-like hold on her bosom had driven some of the sluggishness from her head. Not all of it, certainly, but enough. Feeling the ropes giving under her weight as her progression was restrained by them, she instinctively swung and hooked her arms over the upper strand. When the reverse reaction took place, she was able to reduce the effects of the forward thrust it exerted. Instead of being driven to the centre irresistibly, or thrown to the mat, she was able to keep on her feet and come to a halt still erect.

Ignoring the consternation she noticed on her manager's rat-like face as she glanced in his direction, Tanya strolled across the ring in a leisurely fashion. Still eager to carry on punishing the rash amateur who had given her more trouble than any professional opponent, she was delighted rather than disappointed by the result of the throw. What she believed to have been no more than pure chance had saved her opponent from being bounced to the mat, perhaps sufficiently stunned to be counted out. As it was, she would be able to administer some more suffering. Nor, if the way the other was standing with feet spread apart and shoulders slumped in exhaustion, would she be able to put up any strenuous resistance.

Drawing closer to her opponent, the blonde gave thought to what action would best suit her purpose. She wanted something which would be painful, humiliating, but insufficiently punishing to bring the bout to an immediate end. Knowing from experience in other contests just how much torment could be inflicted upon that portion of the feminine anatomy, she fixed her gaze upon the two heaving mounds beneath her opponent's sweat soaked masculine undershirt. However, as she started to reach for them, another and more severe combination of weakness and a sensation of the room spinning around assailed her. The effect brought her to a halt and she stood still, apart from her hands falling limply to her sides.

Alarm and apprehension tore through Maggie as she realized where the attention of the blonde was being concentrated. She was desperately trying to bring movement to her arms, which seemed to be weighted down with lead, when she saw what was happening. For a moment, she stood motionless and almost uncomprehending. Then some basic instinct informed her that she was being offered an opportunity which was unlikely to be repeated. Sucking in a deep breath and calling upon every last ounce of energy she could command, oblivious of the tumult which rose all around the room at the surprising development, she set about making the most of what she knew from her exhausted condition could be her only chance to stave off defeat.

Maggie had never before engaged upon so strenuous and demanding a type of activity, not even the work she carried out in the forge, but she possessed a sturdy spirit which revolted against the prospect of suffering defeat at the hands of another woman; particularly one who had treated her in such a fashion. Her resolution to avoid this was backed by an affinity for and enjoyment of wrestling which stemmed from her childhood. Being the only sister of five lusty brothers, she had grown up as a tomboy and was an active participant in all their scuffles, proving herself more than capable of holding her own. Nor had her marriage to Cyrus Bollinger and the raising of a family caused too great a change in her ways. In addition to accepting her assistance in his work, being a keen and successful wrestler in the catch-as-catch-can style of his antecedents from Lancashire, England, he had taught her all he knew and it had amused them both to have her keep in practice.

Having heard Bollinger boasting of Maggie's prowess after winning a bout he had arranged, Keleney had suggested she should demonstrate it against an opponent he would procure. Being offered the inducement of a sum of money which would be useful in helping to pay off the mortgage owed by her husband to the local bank, she had agreed without realizing exactly what taking part in a bout of the kind envisaged by the town boss would entail. Once it started, she had found herself up against a variety of methods which could not be employed in the catch-as-catch-can style she had been taught. Although she did not know it, the rules were the predecessors of those for the "all-in" bouts such contests would develop into in the future. In spite of her lack of familiarity, as her opponent had discovered, she was a fast learner. On more than one occasion as the bout progressed, she had duplicated a throw, hold, or means of escaping from the latter which had previously been inflicted upon her and was only permissible under the rules of the "new style" wrestling contest.

Nor was Maggie too bewildered and fatigued by her exertions to do so again!

Remembering how she had come close to losing the second fall shortly after its commencement, but wondering whether she would have sufficient strength to duplicate them, Maggie set about trying to achieve a similar sequence of events. While her right hand sank into and grasped the tangled blonde hair, she pivoted and bent her knees. Thrusting her left arm between Tanya's spread apart thighs, she hauled the other across and started to straighten up.

If Maggie had been less engrossed in the physical effort required by what she was doing, she might have wondered why the experienced blonde did not resist when her intentions became apparent. When she herself had found she was being treated in a similar fashion, even without realizing what was coming, she had tried to prevent it. What was more, an observant spectator might have noticed that her opponent seemed to crumple into flaccid immobility as she was making her preparations to implement her scheme.

Conscious only of what she was trying to achieve, Maggie staggered as she lifted the unresisting weight into the air and almost toppled backwards. Calling upon all her flagging endurance, she contrived to remain erect. Then, although she never knew from whence she found the energy, she turned around three times in rapid succession before bending at the waist and catapulting her burden to the mat. Alighting flat on her back, with a sound similar to that of a side of beef being thrown on to the slab in a butcher's shop, Tanya gave not the slightest indication of feeling the impact.

Continuing to act more out of instinct than conscious thought, Maggie managed to control the stagger induced by the removal of the practically dead weight she had been bearing. Then, returning, she fell forward to land across the torso of her supine rival. Having done so, and becoming aware of the ever growing waves of exhaustion which were threatening to engulf her, she waited in an agony of suspense for the blonde to begin struggling. She knew that if the struggles possessed even a fraction of the earlier vigour she could not prevent herself from being dislodged.

Nor, Maggie told herself bitterly, would she be able to resist whatever the "Countess" might decide to do in retaliation!

Watching what was taking place in the ring, oblivious of the doubts assailing the local contender, the crowd fell silent!

Staring as if he could hardly believe his eyes, the referee sank to his knees in front of the women. If any of the spectators had given the matter any attention, the caution he was displaying would have struck them as being understandable. Once before while he was about to perform a similar function, Tanya had surged upwards with such force that she had precipitated Maggie to land upon him. Then, to the delight of the crowd, the blonde had dived on to him and her opponent. After which, he was subjected to being squashed between their well endowed and squirming bodies for several seconds as they struggled with one another.

Nothing of that nature occurred on this occasion!

In fact, the referee reaching to feel and ensure both of the blonde's shoulders were being pressed against the mat was nothing more than a formality!

Tanya lay completely motionless, not even trying to remove the pressure upon her or prevent the count from taking place.

"One! Two! Three!" the referee yelled, the words and the slap of his right palm on the canvas an accompaniment to each number as it was uttered in the otherwise almost noiseless room. Then, patting Maggie on the back, he went on, "All right, Bollinger. It's over and she's beaten. Get up!"

Despite having received the authorization, the local woman remained where she was for several seconds without attempting to obey. Then a realization of what had been said came to her sluggishly operating senses. Hardly able to believe the long and grueling struggle was over, much less that she was victorious, she tried to push herself up. She discovered that none of her limbs were capable of lifting her aching body from the sweat drenched and, apart from the heaving of the bosom, unmoving torso across which she was lying. Trying without avail to even get on to her hands and knees, she felt somebody grasping her arms and she was lifted to her feet. Weakly shaking her head in an attempt to clear it and remove the copious perspiration which was clouding her vision, she found she was being raised by her husband and buxom saloon-girl who had assisted him as her other second.

"Ladies and gentlemen!" the referee yelled. "The winner of the third and deciding fall. Your own Maggie Bollinger!"

"Well now, Sam," Staines remarked as Keleney let out a snort suggestive of anger and stalked away, being naturally observant and having paid attention to everything that had happened in the ring. "Looks like poor old Bull's lost his bet."

"That's what it *looks* like, Trader," agreed the postmaster, whose eyes were no less keen. There was a sardonic timbre to his voice as he continued, "Let's hope he's a good loser."

CHAPTER FIVE

How Come She Got Unconscious

"God damn it to hell!" Daniel "Bull" Keleney thundered, speaking so loudly that his words drowned the *sotto voce* remarks of the two men whose company he had just quit. Striding swiftly towards the ring, he hauled himself on to the apron with the aid of the ropes. Pointing at the motionless blonde, he went on in tones redolent of suspicion, "Something stinks about her losing that way!"

Having been nourishing much the same doubts over the outcome of the wrestling bout and being given such authoritative guidance by so prominent a member of the community, the spectators who had lost money because of the unexpected turn of events, began to shout their concurrence with the town boss's point of view.

The noise being made by the crowd had an ugly note!

To an experienced peace officer, it would have resembled the opening sounds of a mob priming themselves for a lynching!

Strangely, in spite of the suggestion that there might be very serious trouble brewing, not one of the hard-cases hired by Keleney who were scattered around the bar-room of the Bull's Head Saloon and on the balcony which overlooked it showed any sign of coming to join their employer.

"Hey now, Bull!" Cyrus Bollinger protested, looking around with obvious indignation, as he and the buxom saloon-girl continued to hold on to his wife, whose legs were unable to support her unaided. "Are you saying's how my Maggie didn't lick that 'Countess' gal fair 'n' square, damn it?"

"Hell no, Cy!" the town boss replied hurriedly, ducking between the two upper ropes and entering the ring, the question having caused a cessation of the clamour around it. "Of course I'm not!"

Despite knowing there was help close by, Keleney was aware of how the blacksmith felt about his wife, and had no wish to antagonize him.

The town boss had far too much at stake to want trouble from an irate husband, particularly that one!

Almost two inches taller than Keleney and even more bulky, Bollinger was wearing a collarless white shirt—which was tight enough to emphasize the full extent of his Herculean muscular development—Levi's pants and brown boots which bore an unaccustomed shine in honor of the occasion. He had close cropped black hair and nobody, not even a doting mother, could call him handsome although his rugged face had a certain attraction in its ugliness. While his disposition was generally amiable, he was known to be very protective where members of his family were concerned even though most people considered they were well able to take care of themselves. Furthermore, it had long since become established around Grattan that, due to his great strength and ability as a fighter—whether engaged in friendly and sporting competition as a wrestler, or seriously in a roughhouse brawl—he was a man with whom it was extremely unwise to tangle.

"Then what the Sam Hill *did* you mean?" the burly blacksmith wanted to know, showing no sign of being mollified by the declaration from the town boss.

"Nothing disrespectful to Maggie, Cy," Keleney replied in a placatory tone which was unusual for him. "She won fair and square."

"In that case, are you saying the Countess *threw* the fight?" the blonde's manager demanded irately, his accent that of a New Englander, before Bollinger could reply to the town boss's assurance. Entering the ring without waiting for an answer to his own question, he crossed to kneel alongside her and, making a hurried inspection, went on in a tone which had changed from hostility to urgency, "Hey, she's unconscious. Is there a doctor here?"

"Come on in and take a look at her, Doc!" Keleney ordered rather than requested, looking towards the table at which he had been sitting with a few privileged guests prior to going to make his incorrect bet on the result of the wrestling bout. "I want to know how come she got unconscious so god-damned suddenly."

There was a rumble of concurrence from many of the occupants of the bar-room. It suggested that, although they had fallen silent to hear what was said in the ring, they too were far from satisfied with the way in which the bout was terminated.

The man who stood up in answer to the summons for assistance was short, fat, going bald and middle-aged, with a reddened face which suggested he had a well developed liking for hard liquor. Well dressed and exuding an aura of prosperity, he was the only medical practitioner in Dale County. As such, the majority of his work and revenue came from the employees of Keleney's various business interests. While he had the reputation for hurrying any patients in that category back to their respective jobs when they became ill, or sustained an injury at work, he had an engaging character and was popular.

However, something other than friendly feelings caused the rumble of newly commenced talk to die away as Doctor Cornelius Manneheim clambered laboriously into the ring and began to conduct an examination of "Countess" Tanya Bulganin. Knowing how close an associate he was of the town boss, everybody present—particularly those who hoped his findings would produce a reason to have the lost bets annulled—were eager to hear what he discovered.

"Well now," the medical practitioner boomed out, in his usually far from soft New Yorker's voice, resting the head of the motionless still recumbent woman gently on the canvas. From the way he was speaking, it was apparent that, for once when attending some form of entertainment, he was still sober. However, he gave the impression of being somewhat ill-at-ease and his expression as he looked at Keleney implied he believed that his findings would not be to the other's liking. "She's certainly unconscious—!"

"I can see *that* from here!" the town boss declared with asperity.

"And there's a knot as big as a goose egg on the back of her head," Manneheim continued. "Which is how she got that way."

"How's that, Doc?" Keleney asked, in an equally loud tone.

"She couldn't have wrestled with a lump that size on her head, Bull, at least not for very long, or as well as she did," Manneheim explained, standing up and dusting the knees of his striped trousers with his palms. "So she must have collected it when Maggie slammed her down so hard that last time and it was the bang her head took that knocked her out."

"So that's *all* there was to it?" Keleney growled, sounding disappointed.

"Nothing else but *that*, Bull," the doctor confirmed and, although he did not go so far as uttering the actual words, his demeanour suggested he was thinking, "And I wish I could tell you something that you'd rather hear."

"Then it looks like I owe you and the Countess an apology, Mr. Thorne," the town boss asserted, bringing a much less hostile timbre to his loud voice and extending his right hand with a gesture redolent of contrition mixed with magnanimity. "I'm right sorry for what I said. It's just that I got a touch riled thinking how god-damned close I'd come to winning two thousand simoleons from that five hundred I'd put on your gal."

"No offence took on my part, Mr. Keleney," the manager replied, shaking hands and pitching his voice to a level which indicated a desire to ensure his words would be heard outside the ring as well as by the man to whom they were addressed. "None at all. I'm sorry you lost, though."

"Not nearly as sorry as I am!" the town boss claimed, with a resumption of his previous aura of good humor. "It was hard luck on the Countess that she landed the way she did."

"It was," Amos Thorne agreed. "I reckoned she was all fixed to win, but I'll have to admit she could have asked for what she got."

"How come?" Keleney inquired, frowning a little as if his suspicions were being aroused once more.

"She's always a touch over confident. Damned if I haven't

warned her about it more times than I can remember," Thorne
elaborated and waved a bejewelled right hand towards where
Maggie was being helped to her corner of the ring. "This
time, Mrs. Bollinger was way too smart for her."

"I still don't follow you!" Keleney asserted, expressing the
thoughts of many of the spectators.

"She acted like she was all tuckered out and took the
Countess by surprise," the manager clarified. "Which's how
come she let herself be grabbed, lifted and slammed down like
Mrs. Bollinger did to her."

All of the conversation in the ring had been conducted in
tones which carried to every corner of the otherwise silent
bar-room. Wanting to hear what was being said, everybody
except the trio engaged in the discussion had stopped whatever
they were saying or doing. Those at the rear moved closer and
those on the balcony leaned over so as to miss nothing.

If the response being elicited was any guide, what had
transpired was serving to remove the doubts which had arisen
as a result of the hitherto apparently inexplicable way in which
the bout had ended.

Seeing the seemingly pending and inevitable victory of the
blonde turn so suddenly into a defeat and realizing that the
money they had respectively bet on her was lost, the unfortu-
nate speculators had been suspicious over the way in which it
had happened. However, after having expressed the same
doubts which were plaguing them, Keleney's acceptance of
the explanations given by the doctor and the manager struck
them as convincing proof that there had been no skull-duggery
involved. While they would have been disinclined to believe
the unsupported suppositions and protestations of Thorne,
who was a far from uninvolved party in the affair, they were
aware of how friendly Mannaheim was with the town boss and
felt sure he would not have rendered so unfavourable a verdict
unless it was true.

"Well, you heard Doc and Mr. Thorne, folks!" the town
boss bellowed, turning as he was speaking so he could scan
the entire bar-room. "I don't know about you, but I'm *satisfied* even though I've *lost* my bet. If anybody else isn't, let's
hear from you!" Pausing for a few seconds, he continued
when nobody acted upon his suggestion. "All right then, come
on. Give Maggie and the Countess a cheer. Then everybody

go drink their health on the house!"

Fleeting though his scrutiny of each spectator had been, Keleney combined his impressions with their response to his request for the cheers. Listening to them, he found little to spoil his contentment over the way things had progressed.

Having established that he too was a loser and of a greater sum than anybody else was likely to have wagered, the town boss had achieved the result which he had planned. Following up his ready acceptance of what he was told by Manneheim and the blonde's manager, his offer of drinks on the house had added the final touch. None of those who had fallen into his trap were going to be given an opportunity to brood upon how it had happened. They had been dubious of the way in which the result was attained, but now believed only hard luck and bad judgement on the part of the "Countess" was responsible for their misfortunes.

Nothing could have been further from the truth!

Whatever bad judgement had occurred had been on the part of those among the crowd who had accepted the apparently foolish offer to give odds of four to one on the "local gal" winning!

From the moment Keleney had set about organizing the bout, it had been intended that victory would go to Maggie Bollinger. A shrewd judge of human nature, he had realized that only by ensuring this happened could he hope to produce profitable betting on the event. No amount of civic pride would persuade the majority of the spectators to take more than token wagers upon her being able to defeat a woman known to be an experienced professional wrestler.

Not that Maggie had been aware of, or a party to, the arrangement.

Nor had Tanya.

At least, the blonde had not been informed of all the ramifications of the plot. She had been told no more than that, on receiving a signal from Thorne, she was to keep the fight going as long as possible regardless of how severe a drubbing she was giving her opponent. However, knowing her as well as he did, the manager had been disinclined to count upon her following instructions which would not allow her to win. In addition to the pride she had in her ability as a wrestler, he had seen too much of her vindictive nature to trust her once the bout commenced. Should her opponent prove more competent than was anticipated, as had turned out to be the case, he had doubted whether she would remember that she was supposed to lose the bout.

Accepting Thorne's summation, the town boss had concluded that more positive measures would be required to produce the desired result.

These were taken!

The final schooner of beer Tanya had received and emptied, such being an accepted restorative in the course of her bouts, was laced with a "knock-out" potion supplied by Keleney. While the administration was performed without difficulty, there had been a delay before the effects produced results (possibly because she was too excited to suffer the effects). This caused the conspirators some uncomfortable moments, as she had continued to handle her opponent so roughly that there was a danger of her winning before she succumbed.

Fortunately, Maggie had had sufficient courage and stamina for her to survive until she was able to take advantage of the dazed condition induced upon the blonde by the noxious draught. It had been a very close thing, but there was an added bonus for the town boss. Pure chance had led her to apply the finishing touches to her already unconscious opponent in a fashion which allowed what passed as a feasible explanation for the way it had come about.

Nobody had had the temerity to ask to see the bump on the back of Tanya's head, which did not exist outside of Manneheim's fake diagnosis, so they were unaware that her condition was produced by means other than those described. What was more, the "sporting" acceptance of Keleney that Maggie had won "fairly," his "apology" to the unconscious blonde's manager and the offer of a free drink on the house had combined to divert the losers from their already shaken suspicions.

Generous as the latter inducement might be, however, it was far less so than appeared on the surface. Not only had its maker acquired a large sum as a result of the misguided wagers, the free drinks would lead to the purchase of others which would more than recover the loss of revenue arising from his "largesse".

There was, nevertheless, one fly to mar the ointment of the town boss's self-satisfaction!

Having studied Samuel Williams and Walter "Trader"

Staines in passing, Keleney was disturbed by their attitude. While he was sure neither had been taken in by the explanation which had convinced everybody else, this was not what he was finding worrying. Even if they had made wagers, which he knew was not the case, they would be too wise to express their doubts publicly. It was the memory of the conversation he had been having with them during the final seconds of the bout which was causing his concern.

Unless Keleney was mistaken, neither man had been puzzled or alarmed by the failure of Orville Webster to put in an appearance. Nor was this merely restricted to his absence from the saloon. When he had not shown up at the home of one or the other, being eager to learn what he had discovered about the fake trial, it seemed logical that they would have gone in search of him.

Yet neither had done so!

Even if one or the other dissident had eluded the men sent by the town boss to prevent Webster from reaching them, it was unlikely he could have discovered what was happening at the schoolhouse—whether the killing, or merely the preparations to give the impression a robbery had taken place—without being detected by Brick Shatterhouse and Moses Broody. Or, should either had done so he would have informed his companion. In which case, Keleney doubted whether they could have appeared so completely at ease and unresentful in his company. Certainly they would not have been so calm if they were aware of the schoolteacher's murder.

Suddenly, the town boss began to surmise something of the true state of affairs!

The possibility that Webster had arrived at the valley by chance and was not there at the instigation of either dissident failed to arouse the slightest remorse in Keleney over having ordered his execution. If the theory was correct, his death would still prove beneficial in the effect it would have upon the education of the children. Furthermore, providing he was not investigating the fake trial on behalf of Staines, the intended betting coup would not be adversely affected. As long as his presence at the race course remained unknown to Williams and the owner of the livery barn, they were unlikely to suspect the trick which had been played upon the latter.

While drawing his far from displeasing conclusions,

Keleney glanced over the heads of the crowd to the door of his private office. It was closed, but a frown came to his face as he noticed that the sliding panel he used for purposes of unsuspected observation when inside was drawn back. As he gave a sharp and angry jerking motion with his head, it slid across, apparently of its own volition, to conceal the opening.

Instead of leaving the ring to investigate the phenomenon, being aware of what was portended by it, the town boss went to where the saloon-girl and Bollinger were ministering to Maggie, who was still in a state of great exhaustion. Asking after her welfare and being informed that she would not require attention from Manneheim, he promised her husband she would receive a bonus for the excellence of her performance. Then, suggesting the couple and their assistant should be his guests for the rest of the evening, he went over to pass a similar invitation to Thorne.

Just as Keleney was on the point of leaving the ring, something happened which brought him to a halt!

The interruption was not unexpected by the town boss!

It had, in fact, been brought about by the angry signal Keleney had directed at the open observation flap of his private office!

Having been reminded of the orders he had received, for he had been too engrossed by what was happening in the ring to be carrying them out, Hawley Grenville had left the office by its second entrance. Hurrying along the side alley to the front of the saloon, he threw open the batwing doors and burst into the bar-room.

Tall, grey haired and in his late forties, Grenville had the physique of a once powerful athlete now run to seed as a result of far too much good living and addiction to the pleasures of the flesh. However, he was otherwise a distinguished and commanding figure. As always, he was dressed in the height of western city fashion and the Colt Civilian Model Peacemaker, in the fast draw holster of a black gunbelt so well polished it looked like patent leather, had a fancy silver inlaid ivory handle.

All in all, despite serving in the dual capacity of town marshal for Grattan and sheriff of Dale County, the peace officer's attire was more expensive than could be supported even by his combined salary from both offices. This surprised nobody in the region. It was common knowledge that, the oaths he had sworn when being appointed to both positions notwithstanding, he was Keleney's man body and soul.

"Bull!" Grenville announced as he crossed the threshold. Possessing a stentorian voice, which he was employing to its full potential, it sounded over the wave of conversation that had been resumed following the offer of drinks on the house. Everybody looked in his direction.

"What is it?" the town boss shouted back, although he had no need to ask the question other than for the sake of appearances.

"Somebody's killed the schoolteacher!" the peace officer replied and, to give the impression he had just made the discovery, he went on, "I found him as I was making my rounds and reckoned you'd want to know!"

CHAPTER SIX

Get The Bastard Who Killed Him!

"Oh my god, Sam!" Walter "Trader" Staines gasped, his attention diverted from a sardonic scrutiny of what was taking place in the bar-room of the Bull's Head Saloon. "Did you hear that?"

"I couldn't help but hear it!" Samuel Williams confirmed, in no less startled and disturbed tones, also having swung his gaze towards Town Marshal Hawley Grenville.[1] "Come on. Let's find out how it happened and who did it!"

Being intelligent and observant men, who had learned the advisability of possessing a healthy scepticism with regard to any activity organized by Daniel "Bull" Keleney, the pair had not been taken in by the events which had followed the surprise ending of the wrestling bout. Their suspicions had already been aroused by hearing the nearest gambler offer odds of four to one, and by noticing that others heard the apparently unsubstantiated supposition that Maggie Bollinger

1 *Although the post of sheriff—granting jurisdiction throughout the whole of Dale County—was ostensibly more important than that of town marshal, whose authority was restricted to the city limits of Grattan, we will continue to refer to Hawley Grenville in the latter capacity for purposes of clarity. J.T.E.*

would be the winner. Nor had they changed their point of view when the town boss had denied that the seemingly misguided gamblers were in his employ. This had merely served to make them consider their doubts were fully justified.

Paying far greater attention than any of the other spectators, Williams and Staines had noticed that "Countess" Tanya Bulganin had started to display symptoms of dizziness and uncertainty on her feet shortly after drinking the beer she was given by her manager. They had also seen how she was beginning to collapse, in a manner suggestive of a loss of consciousness, just before she was raised across the shoulders of her opponent. She had also been unnaturally limp and unresisting while being twirled around and dropped, despite the fact that her experience was sufficient to warn her what was coming.

Although the pair were willing to concede that the blonde could have banged her head on landing, because of what had immediately preceded it, they were certain this was not the cause of her comatose condition. Nor had the diagnosis by Doctor Cornelius Manneheim caused them to revise their belief that she had been drugged and was in, or very close to, such a state before she arrived on the mat. They were too aware of the close connections between the local medical practitioner and Keleney to be willing to accept such an apparently adverse explanation at its face value. The fact that Manneheim had refrained from drinking—which, to his credit, was his habit when expecting a call to be made upon his professional services—had merely served to strengthen their convictions.

However, in spite of having deduced that the town boss had once again succeeded in making dupes out of a number of his employees, Williams and Staines were too wise to attempt an exposure of the betting coup. They did not doubt he had taken adequate precautions to ensure such a contingency would be dealt with swiftly. What was more, aided by the good will he had built up during the evening, it would be prevented in such a fashion that the crowd would have no sympathy for, nor be willing to give credence to, any adverse comments.

The announcement made by the town marshal on his arrival came as such a shock. It drove all thoughts of how the trickery had been carried out from the heads of the two dissidents!

Despite the conclusions drawn by Keleney as he was standing in the ring, Williams and Staines had been aware of Orville Webster's absence. They had not, however, been alarmed or disturbed by his failure to join them.

Not only had the young schoolteacher expressed a certain disenchantment with the prospect of attending the wrestling bout between Maggie and the "Countess," but the pair had known of his intention to go on a walk to continue studying the local flora and fauna. Being aware of his absorbing interest in such matters and remembering other occasions when he had remained on the range for long periods if he became engrossed with something out of the ordinary, they had concluded the same thing had happened which accounted for him not arriving in the bar-room.

As the postmaster and the owner of the livery barn had not joined the general rush for the bar to partake in the "largesse" offered by the town boss, they had no difficulty in acting upon the former's suggestion. They were just starting to walk towards Keleney and the peace officer when a thought came to Williams. It was something he had noticed earlier, in fact, but the full significance of it had eluded him until that moment.

While there were several of the hard-cases hired by the town boss present as usual—either in the bar-room proper, or strategically positioned on the balcony which overlooked it—the two upon whom he placed most reliance were missing!

Yet, with the possibility of serious trouble breaking out if the unexpected result of the wrestling bout was contested by those who lost bets, Brick Shatterhouse and Moses Broody should have been on the premises!

Only something of even greater importance would have compelled Keleney to dispense with the services of that particular pair of hard-cases!

Furthermore, Williams knew something of the nature of the marshal!

It was most surprising, the postmaster considered, that Grenville was so conscientious in his duties that he was walking the rounds personally when such an attractive entertainment as the wrestling match between two shapely and scantily dressed women was taking place!

Added to the abstinence being shown by Manneheim and the absence of Keleney's two top hard-cases, Williams found the behaviour of the peace officer most disturbing!

"All right, Hawley," Keleney greeted, glancing at the approaching pair of dissidents, although he paid no attention whatsoever to the other occupants of the bar-room who were also moving forward to listen. "How and where did it happen?"

"Down to the schoolhouse, Bull, lying by the front door," Grenville replied, reversing the order in which the information was requested. "He'd been robbed and shot in the back."

"Who did it?" the town boss demanded and the crowd rumbled just as angrily as when joining in his "protests" over the way the bout had ended.

"I don't *know*, damn it!" the peace officer admitted, with such apparent heat and sincerity he might have been speaking the truth. "It was the first time I'd got out that way this evening and there wasn't anybody inside the school, or anywhere around it, when I got there and found him."

"Isn't there any god-damned thing to give you a notion of who did it?" Keleney challenged, putting on an equally convincing display of concern.

"I didn't wait to look for clues," Grenville answered, never one to miss an opportunity to remind others that he was an experienced peace officer, even though he knew his continuance in office depended solely upon the town boss rather than the whim of the voters of the community. "As soon as I saw what had happened, I came straight over here to tell you about it."

"Then, by god, you'd best go straight back *there* and find out who the son-of-a-bitch was that did it!" Keleney boomed. "I know we didn't allus see eye to eye about stuffing kids' heads full of useless book-learning and such, but I liked young Webster a lot and I'm telling you to do *everything* you can to get the bastard who killed him!"

"Count on *me* for that, Bull!" Grenville promised, once again contriving to sound as if he meant what he was saying even though he was aware that the last thing wanted by the town boss was for the murderers to be identified, much less apprehended.

"I know I can, Hawley, and so does everybody else,"

Keleney asserted. "But, if you need *any* help at all, just say the word and, whatever it might be and I can get it for you, it's yours."

"Maybe you should have Brick Shatterhosue and Moe Broody to go lend Hawley a hand, Bull," Williams suggested, watching for any response elicited by the suggestion. "They've been his deputies afore now, I mind."

"I'll send out to my place and have them come if you want them, Hawley," the town boss offered, despite knowing the pair were in the living quarters upstairs at the saloon. He had darted a quick look at the elderly postmaster before speaking, seeing only what would pass to most people as a desire to render helpful advice. Aware that this was unlikely to be the case and wondering how much the other knew, or merely suspected, he went on, "With the race coming up tomorrow and being so sure he's going to win, I've got them out there keeping an eye on old Black Prince."

"There's no need for you to send for them, in that case, Bull," Grenville refused. "I'll go to the schoolhouse now and take a closer look around. Then, if it's needed, I reckon I won't be short of volunteers to ride in a posse."

"Mind if Trader and me go along with Hawley, Bull?" Williams requested, his attitude implying he believed such authorization would be required. "Young Orville was a real good friend of our'n as well's your'n and we could maybe help a mite."

"It's up to Hawley, not me, him being the marshal," Keleney answered, trying as he always did when there was an audience to convey the impression that the peace officer was a free agent. However, as he did not wish to leave Grenville with any doubts over his sentiments in the matter, he continued, "But I don't see why you *shouldn't* go. Do you, Hawley?"

"No," the marshal confirmed, drawing the correct conclusion and, although he would have preferred to keep the two elderly men out of the affair, going along with the wishes of the town boss. "Th—You might's well come with me, Sam, Trader."

"Why thank you 'most to death," Williams drawled, his voice only mildly sardonic. "We're right obliged. Aren't we, Trader?"

"Obliged's the word for it, Sam," replied the owner of the livery barn, ensuring that no more than a slight timbre of sarcasm tinged his tone.

"I'll come aong with you as well, Hawley," Keleney declared rather than suggested. Wanting to find out the extent of the two dissidents' suspicions or knowledge, he was disinclined to accept a summation at secondhand, even though it would be coming from a man most people might consider well qualified to draw a reasonably accurate conclusion. "Unless you've got any objections, that is?"

"None at all, Bull," Grenville assented immediately, which did not come as any great surprise to the majority of the listening crowd. "You'd best come with us, Doc, and you, Melvin."

"Sure, Hawley," answered the undertaker, Melvin Caine, and Manneheim also signified agreement.

"All you folks go on with what you were doing!" Keleney commanded, swinging his gaze around the crowd. "From what I knew of him, I reckon that's what young Webster would want you to do."

"He was never a spoilsport, Bull!" confirmed one of the men who had frequently harassed Webster so as to curry favour with the town boss.

"That's one thing *nobody* could ever call him," Keleney agreed and raised his voice. "Hey, Bernie!"

"Yeah, boss?" replied the chief of the bartenders.

"Give everybody another free drink to raise to the memory of a damned good schoolteacher," the town boss instructed, knowing the gesture would be beneficial in distorting the memories any of the customers had about the way in which his men had treated Webster. "I reckon that's the least we can do in his honour, except for getting the bastard who killed him."

Exchanging glances, neither the postmaster nor the owner of the livery barn needed to put into words the fact that apprehending the killer was the last thing Keleney wanted!

The pair were mutually determined to do all they could to see the murderer of the schoolteacher brought to justice and, hopefully, find a connection which would help free Grattan from the clutches of the town boss.

• • •

"*Everything* points to young Webster having been killed by whoever was robbing the schoolhouse," Town Marshal Hawley Grenville announced, in a tone which indicated he considered there could be no argument against his summation. "He must have come on them while they were doing it and they gunned him down when they saw he was running out to fetch me."

Listening to the declaration being made by the peace officer and watching the body of their young friend being removed by the undertaker's men, Sam Williams and Trader Staines were alike in their dissatisfaction with his conclusions.

Having been born and grown up through the violent early years of Texas' existence, neither of the dissidents was a stranger to death in all its forms. In fact, each had lost somebody close to him as a result of violence. While they were sorrowed and infuriated by the murder of Orville Webster, they had not allowed their emotions to cloud their judgement. Nor had their grief served to diminish the keenness of their perceptions and, without consultation between themselves, they had formed almost identical impressions from what they had seen and been told.

While Doctor Manneheim and the undertaker were engaged upon their respective duties, Grenville had carried out an examination of the premises. His activities might have impressed an observer who was unaware of the true state of affairs, but he was far less successful than he would have wished in convincing Williams and Staines that he was performing the task with the intention of solving the crime. Following him, they could not complain about the vigour he exhibited. On the other hand, neither was surprised by the almost negative results of his efforts. He had pointed out and remarked upon the all too plain indications—such as the absence of the silver sporting trophies—that a robbery had taken place, but had attached no significance to the broken photograph lying on the floor. Nor had he given any sign of realizing that the spent cartridge he had picked up might offer an important clue. Instead, acting as if the discovery was a major achievement, he had pointed out the broken window of the living quarters as being the way access to the premises had been attained.

Despite the doubts each was feeling, neither the postmaster

nor the owner of the livery barn had questioned the accuracy of the statement made by the doctor after he had studied the body. At the completion of his no more than perfunctory tests, he had asserted that the murder took place somewhat later than they surmised was the case from what they had seen of its condition. They had realized the discrepancy was intended to provide an alibi for the killer, should one be needed, but felt sure they would get nowhere by making their suppositions known to the men about them. To do so would achieve nothing more than to confirm their suspicions to Keleney and they knew that it might lead him to take positive measures to ensure their silence. They could do nothing to avenge their young friend if they too were killed.

However, despite having seen nothing to suggest more than one person was involved, Williams' suspicions over the absence of Brick Shatterhouse and Moses Broody would not allow him to let the pronouncement of the peace officer pass unchallenged.

"*Them?*" the postmaster queried. "How many of *them* were there?"

"I don't know," Grenville answered, suddenly realizing he had inadvertently made a slip of the tongue. "It was just a figure of speech, damn it!"

"Hell's fires, Hawley!" Keleney protested, not caring for the way in which the peace officer had responded to the question. "Nobody from Grattan, nor anywhere else around Dale County would have done it!"

"I'd say the same, Bull," the marshal seconded.

"Have there been any strangers around?" the town boss hinted.

"No—!" Grenville began, but realized this was not the answer expected of him and thought for a moment. "Hell, yes. There *has* been. I forgot all about *them* for the moment, Bull!"

"Who?" Keleney inquired, pleased that the peace officer had finally remembered something told to him when preparing for the investigation he was now carrying out.

"There were a couple of saddle-bums drifted in this morning," Grenville replied. "They were out back of the Overland corral when I come on them and, as they couldn't give an account of what they were doing, I told them to get the hell out of town. Only it could be I ought to have jailed them, instead of letting them go."

"How come?" Staines inquired, despite feeling sure he could guess the answer.

"They allowed to be damned close to the blanket," the marshal replied, as the owner of the livery barn had anticipated, using a gambling term for one who was almost out of funds. "And they looked mean enough not to be too choosy how they got back into the chips."

"I mind seeing them," Williams remarked. "Only I don't recollect neither of them toting one of the new model rifles's Winchester've not long brought out."

"What makes you think they did have?" Keleney challenged, being unaware that the comment had any significance as he had not been informed of Broody's failure to retrieve the damning piece of evidence.

"Looks like you didn't see that empty shell Hawley picked up," the postmaster answered, having made the identification before the peace officer had pocketed the spent cartridge case without giving it the attention it deserved. "Unless I'm tolerable mistaken, which I'll have to admit I've been on occasion, it was one of them new forty-four-forty[2] hulls this latest Winchester takes 'stead of rim-fires like the Old Yellowboy uses."[3]

"Maybe you'd best take a look and make sure, Hawley," Staines suggested, his demeanour redolent of helpfulness. "Like Sam says, he's been wrong afore."

"I don't need to look," the marshal declared and, despite being aware of what was implied by the information, he tried to give the impression of dismissing it as having no significance. "It is one, but I don't see why they shouldn't be toting one of the new Winchesters."

"Price I saw being asked for them was betwixt thirty-eight and sixty dollars," Williams explained. "Which same'd make it a pretty expensive sort of a gun for a couple of close-to-the-blanket saddle-bums to be toting, I'd say."

"By golly, Hawley, Sam's *right!*" Keleney claimed, despite his concealed fury over Broody having made such a potentially dangerous mistake. Looking straight at the peace officer, he went on in a noticeably pointed manner, "Have you heard

2 *"Forty-four-forty:"* a cartridge with a bullet of .44 calibre and a charge of forty grains of powder. J.T.E.

3 *"Old Yellowboy:"* the nickname given to the Winchester Model of 1866 rifle on account of its brass frame. J.T.E.

of one of them being *stolen* anywhere heareabouts recently?"

"No—!" Grenville commenced, but once again surmised from the glare he received that an answer in the affirmative was being sought, and made a hurried revision. Slapping his left hand on his thigh in a theatrical gesture, he went on, "Damn it, *yes*. I have, though. I was talking to one of the deputies when I was down to Karnes City on Wednesday and he reckoned he'd heard somebody over to De Witt County had robbed a drummer and took one of them new Winchesters in the booty. Allowed it was a couple of saddle-bums did it."

"But you said neither of that pair had one with him," Staines pointed out in what might have passed as an artless desire to be of assistance, although neither the town boss nor the peace officer considered it was intended as such.

"He wouldn't have brought it in with him, happen he knew there was a lawman as smart as Hawley here," Keleney offered, seeing the marshal was clearly at a loss to know what response to make for the best. "'Specially if they was scouting the town for some place to rob."

"Did they know about you, Hawley?" Williams inquired.

"Well, yes, they'd heard some about me," Grenville replied, adopting a tone he hoped would suggest modesty combined with conviction. "At least, that's what I figured, way they talked when I called them down."

"Don't look like they took what they heard to heart, though," the postmaster commented, wishing he had been able to eavesdrop upon the conversation he had seen taking place at the rear of his establishment prior to the expulsion of the two men in question. "Only that could be 'cause they wasn't any too smart, looks to me."

"What're you getting at, Sam?" Keleney wanted to know, trying to prevent his growing asperity from becoming too obvious.

"Only trying to figure things out," Williams asserted blandly. "Way it looks to me—and I reckon's how Hawley'll've beaten me to getting there—they'd find a heap more places than here around town it'd pay 'em to rob."

"They wouldn't've been empty like the schoolhouse," the marshal objected and, as he did so, realized he had once more made a remark at odds with an earlier statement. Hoping it had gone unnoticed, he went on, "At least, going by the way he was dressed, I'd say young Webster had been out on the range, watching animals and such like he does and'd only just come back. Which being, they'd find the schoolhouse empty where most other places likely wouldn't be."

"That could be," the postmaster conceded, mentally accepting there was nothing more than his own still unproven suspicions to discount the theory.

"Anyways, it must have been those two saddle-bums, or somebody else who'd come into town looking for somebody to rob," Grenville continued, sensing from the concession that he had gained a breakthrough—if not a complete victory— and wanting to strengthen it. "Young Webster didn't have any enemies around here that I've heard tell of. But *you* knew him better than I did. Has he ever mentioned he had any?"

"Can't say he has," Williams admitted.

"How about maybe somebody being after him from his home town?" Keleney suggested.

"He never let on about it to us if there should be," Williams admitted and Staines signified concurrence.

"Then it *had* to be somebody's was looking for some place to rob!" the marshal declared. "And those saddle-bums're the only strangers who've been around recently."

"You'd best take out a posse and see happen you can pick up the trail of whoever did it, Hawley," the town boss said, more as an order than a suggestion. "It's no use going afore morning, though. Ask for some fellers to ride with you when we get back to the saloon. You won't be short of volunteers, I'd reckon."

"I won't," Grenville agreed, knowing he would have several of the hard-cases assigned in case he needed them. "Maybe you and Trader want to come along, Sam?"

"Not me, Hawley," Williams refused, knowing the posse would achieve nothing unless the two saddle-bums should have the misfortune to be found by them and be killed to remove suspicion from the men he believed were really responsible. "I've got a stage coming in and the mail to get ready for going out on it."

"I've got too much on at the barn," Staines seconded, duplicating his companion's summations. "Hey though. What about the race tomorrow?"

"What about it?" Keleney asked.

"Are you still going to run it?" the owner of the livery barn inquired.

"Sure," the town boss affirmed, but his attitude implied that he had not given the matter any thought until that moment. "I don't reckon young Webster would want all those folks who're looking forward to it to be disappointed. But if *you* reckon that's the way he'd want it, I'll go along with what *you* say."

"I reckon you're right, Bull," Williams stated, being too wily to allow the onus for cancelling the eagerly awaited race to be placed upon himself and Staines. "He wouldn't want it stopped. So you go ahead with it."

"Sure," the owner of the livery barn went on. "Maybe this time there'll be a hoss show up's can lick your old Black Prince, Bull."

CHAPTER SEVEN

A Good *Amigo* of Ole Devil Hardin

"Howdy, boss," Moses Broody greeted, rising from the table at which he and Brick Shatterhouse were drinking whiskey and playing cribbage, as—followed by Town Marshal Hawley Grenville—the owner of the Bull's Head Saloon came into the luxurious living accommodation he maintained on the first floor. "Did everything go off all right down to the school-house?"

Even as he was asking the question, the hard-case noticed the angry expression on the face of his employer and concluded that the answer was unlikely to be in the affirmative!

Yet, although Broody did not know it, the town boss had been in an amiable and satisfied mood until a few minutes earlier!

Despite being aware that Samuel Williams and Walter "Trader" Staines suspected he was implicated in the murder of Orville Webster, Daniel "Bull" Keleney had felt sure there was no way they could establish his guilt. In fact, so great had been his assurance on the point, he had accepted without argument their suggestion that they remained at the school-house to pack the dead man's belongings for shipment to his parents. Although Keleney had instructed one of the pair of hard-cases—who had accompanied him ostensibly to help the undertaker—to keep them under observation without being detected, he had considered the surveillance was no more than a precaution taken as a matter of course and there was no real need for it to be necessary.

On the town boss and the peace officer returning to the saloon, the curiosity of the crowd was sufficient to halt their celebrations. Leaving Grenviille to do the talking, Keleney had been satisfied with the evidence that his "largesse" was paying the anticipated dividends. Their feelings of remorse over the murder of the schoolteacher notwithstanding, it was clear that the customers had not allowed the festivities to diminish in his absence. Nevertheless, they kept silent while being informed of the discoveries made at the schoolhouse and, as expected, there had been no shortage of volunteers when the marshal announced he would be taking out a posse in the morning to search for the murderers.

With that aspect over and the interrupted activities recommenced, Keleney had set about laying the foundations for a future betting coup. After talking quietly with Amos Thorne and learning that "Countess" Tanya Bulganin was still unconscious, he had called for silence. Knowing him, this was soon attained and he announced what everybody else believed to have been the subject under discussion.

Saying how much he had enjoyed the wrestling bout and receiving a tumultuous agreement from his audience, the town boss suggested a return contest would prove equally satisfying. When the roar of concurrence died down, the manager (as he had been instructed) declared that the "Countess" would be unable to oblige as she was fully committed for several weeks ahead. Jovially disputing the shouts that she was "scared of taking another whupping," he had offered an alternative solution. Although he would bring her back to Grattan when at liberty to do so, it was possible another contender could be found in the meantime. Her next bout was against Big Ann Derby in Brownsville the following Saturday. Provided Maggie Bollinger was in agreement, Thorne would see if the other professional woman wrestler would accept a challenge.

The manager's suggestion had been met with great enthusiasm, even on the part of those who had lost money as a result of the "unexpected" victory by the local woman. Faced with the eagerness being displayed all around her and the offer of a much larger sum in recompense by Keleney, as well as having found the acclaim to which she had been subjected since winning most satisfying, Maggie had agreed. She had also promised to go into strict training, so as to be in even better physical condition when matched against her next opponent. Having gained her acceptance, the town boss had promised to arrange for the bout to take place in four weeks time.

Although the man left on watch by Keleney had arrived soon after the betting coup was prepared, saying Williams and Staines were conducting an investigation of their own at the schoolhouse, he had not at first been perturbed. He had expected they would behave in such a fashion and believed they would meet no greater success than previously. The equanimity had been rudely shattered by Grenville remarking that, while the two dissidents had failed to duplicate the discovery, he had found splashes of blood from Shatterhouse's nose on the floor of the living quarters.

Possessing a greater respect than the peace officer for the pair's powers of observation, the town boss was barely able to conceal his fury over not having been warned of the matter earlier. If he had known, although he could not have refused to let them stay behind, he would have ensured they were unable to carry out a sufficiently thorough examination to allow them to learn of the injury sustained by the hard-case.

Ordering the marshal to accompany him, Keleney had been in a far from amiable frame of mind as he went to his living quarters. Nor was his temper improved by finding the two men responsible for his dilemma relaxing and partaking of his best whiskey as if they had carried out their task in a completely satisfactory manner.

"If it did," the town boss answered heatedly, confirming Broody's suppositions with regards to his mood. "It's no god-damned thanks to you two."

"Us, boss?" the hard-case asked and Shatterhouse showed an equal puzzlement.

"*You!*" Keleney confirmed and selected the speaker as his first target. "Why the hell didn't you pick up that 'mother-something' empty case instead of leaving the son-of-a-bitch lying on the floor?"

"Don't tell me you left it behind, Moe?" asked Shatter-house, whose already far from attractive nose was now considerably swollen and inflamed. Sensing something was seriously amiss, he was hoping that all the blame would be confined to his companion's omission. "What for'd you do a fool thing like that?"

"Because I couldn't think of *everything* and you wasn't being a god-damned bit of help, moaning your nose was busted and splashing blood all around the god-damned room!" Broody answered with asperity, being equally desirous and avoiding recriminations over the errors they might have committed. Realizing he had made a potentially serious mistake, his voice took on a note of contrition as he addressed his irate employer, "I'm sorry I left it, boss. But I figured's how we'd best get out and away from there as quick's we could, seeing's how Brick was bleeding like a stuck shoat, in case anybody should've heard the shot and come. Anyways, one empty shell's no different from another of the same kind."

"Except there aren't half a dozen of those god-damned new Winchesters in all of Dale County for it to be different from!" Keleney spat out, pointing with a savage gesture to where the rifle in question was leaning in a corner of the comfortably furnished room. "You stay out of sight until that nose looks right again, Brick. And don't *you* go showing that 'mother-something' gun to *anybody* around town, Broody!"

"Especially to Sam Williams, Trader Staines, or any of their bunch," supplemented the marshal.

"Those two old bastards—!" Broody commenced derisively, having noticed the use of his surname and hoping to exculpate himself in the eyes of his employer.

"Were slick enough to know just what kind of 'mother-something' empty case it was *you'd* left behind!" the town boss interrupted viciously.

"They don't know we done it though, boss," Shatterhouse growled, showing concern. "Do they?"

"How the hell could they know, seeing—!" Broody questioned, but once again was not allowed to elaborate.

"They might not *know,*" Keleney inserted in a tone of warning. "But they sure as shit soon started asking where you pair were when they heard the schoolteacher'd been killed. So

I want you two out of town and sight for a while, until this blows over."

"Sounds like it's starting to rain," Grenville remarked, as a rapid pattering noise on the window made itself heard. "If it's as heavy as last night, I'll be able to call off taking out the posse in the morning."

"Who after?" Broody inquired, his attitude wary and suspicious.

"Nobody in particular," the marshal answered, guessing what had motivated the question. "We made out we thought he was gunned down by somebody from out of town and I've said I'm taking a posse, making out we'll be hunting for whoever did it. Only, with this rain, I'll be able to tell them any tracks'll've been washed away and there's no point in us wasting time doing it."

"Sure," Keleney went on approvingly, thinking of the possibility that some of his intended victims might be on the posse and feel so obligated to the memory of the dead schoolteacher that they would stay on their quest until it was too late for them to reach the valley and bet on the quarter horse race. "And I'll see that they go along with you when you tell them."

"That's all very well, boss!" Broody protested, coming as close as he dared to displaying asperity towards a decision supported by his employer. "But, if those two old bastards *know* about Brick and me—!"

"They don't *know* anything!" the town boss corrected. However, as he realized he might be pushing the two hard-cases too hard and which might prove inadvisable, he forced himself to go in a much less hostile fashion, "Don't worry, boys. All they are is *suspicious*."

"And, as long as *I'm* handling the investigation," Grenville supported confidently, "that's all they will be."

"I can't say's how I'm took with the notion of having them even *suspicious* about me!" Broody objected sullenly. Being aware that, as he was the one who had fired the fatal shot, he would be the most endangered of those present if the murder of the schoolteacher was brought home to him, he considered he had the most to lose. However, suspecting that to present such a point of view might invoke severe repercussions, he refrained from mentioning it and continued, "Those two old bastards have been putting a burr under your saddle for years, boss. I don't know why you haven't had both of them made wolf bait long afore now."[1]

"That wouldn't be any too smart," Shatterhouse claimed, with the superior air of one who was explaining a point which the other should not have overlooked. "Or have you forgot how Williams's allus letting on's how he's such a good *amigo* of Ole Devil Hardin, Moe?"

"Do *you* reckon's he is, boss?" Broody inquired, incensed by his companion's condescending attitude, but under no illusion of the potential danger posed by the man claimed as a good friend by the postmaster.

"I don't know," the town boss confessed. "Parry's never seen any letters's've passed between them since he started working there."

"Then it might only be a bluff," Broody hinted, unwilling to surrender his attempt to bring about the removal of what he considered was a threat to his life and knowing that— although employed as assistant to Williams—Terry Parry received payment from Keleney to act as a spy on the dissidents.

"I don't give a shit whether it's a bluff or not!" the town boss stated emphatically. "Williams's the postmaster and I'm not about to take the chance of doing *anything* that could pass as tampering with the mails. That's Federal trouble and there's some in this god-damned town who'd like nothing better than to have an excuse to bring a U.S. marshal nosing around."

"That's true enough," Grenville seconded, his demeanour that of a schoolteacher delivering an explanation to a couple of far from intelligent pupils. "After the fuss made by Bull's *amigo* in the State Legislature, when I complained about those two Rangers who came in without me asking for them after the stage hold up we had, they'll steer clear of us.[2] But we

---

1 *"Made wolf bait"*: *cowhands' term meaning to kill. It was derived from one of the methods used in the Old West for dealing with carnivores not necessarily just wolves, which preyed on livestock. An animal would be killed and, having its body impregnated with poison, was left on the range to be eaten by the predators. J.T.E.*

2 *Although, as we recorded in* A TOWN CALLED YELLOW DOG *Texas Rangers sometimes acted upon reports from private individuals*

tance. Knowing that sending the letter without Keleney learning of it would not be a straightforward matter, he had written
an account of the conditions which prevailed in Grattan and
told of his suspicions with regards to the murder of the schoolteacher. He had finished by asking if help could be sent to
gather proof of Keleney's complicity and avenge Webster's
death.

Having dispatched the mail which was awaiting collection
on the north-bound stagecoach, Williams had left Terry Parry
to attend to his dual businesses and had gone out to the valley.
Meeting Staines, who had arrived earlier with the intention of
checking the suspicions which had taken form on learning that
Ezekiel Barnesley had been spreading the story about the
"trial" they had witnessed, he had barely done more than
exchange a greeting when there was another request for information on the subject.

"There's no call for you to be playing it so god-damned
close to your vest!" protested the seeker of verification, once
again duplicating the reaction of his predecessors—if not with
the identical words—on receiving a similarly unproductive
response from Staines. "I got told secret-like that you'd seen
that bay, Three Socks, being run along the course yesterday
and he's faster over it than the Prince."

"Who told you?" the owner of the livery barn inquired,
although previous experiences had not been such that he
expected to receive the answer he required.

"I promised I wouldn't say," the man declared, as had the
others. "How about it, Trader?"

"Well now," Staines replied, despite having learned the
futility of trying to dissuade those who had approached him.
"The time *was* a mite faster, I'll have to admit. But leave us
not forget it rained last night and the Prince always runs better
on a soft track."

"It'd rained just as heavy the night afore last," the man
pointed out testily, clearly drawing the same conclusions with
regards to the motives behind the evasive answers as had his
predecessors. "Damn it all, Trader. We've been doing business together for *years*. You ought to know you can tell *me*.
I'll spread my money around so it won't bring the odds down
for *you*. All I want from you is to know if Three Socks is
better than the Prince."

"He made better time *yesterday*," Staines conceded with a

sigh, knowing it would be futile to lie. However, playing for time, he went on, "But—!"

The ploy failed!

"The race'll be starting soon!" the man interrupted, grinning broadly. "I'd best go and start putting my money down. By god, it'll be a real pleasure to play Bull at his own game and beat him!"

"I hope he still feels that way when it's over," Williams commented dryly, as he and the owner of the livery barn watched the optimistic gambler hurrying away.

"So do I," Staines replied. "But I'd be willing to bet he won't be."

"Did you find anything?" Williams asked, glancing towards the crowd which was lining the race course.

"I didn't even get a chance to *look,*" Staines replied. "There were too many of Bull's hard-cases around when I got here."

"But you still reckon the trial you saw was rigged?"

"I'm damned sure it was!"

"The way you said?"

"It most likely was," the owner of the livery barn asserted, having made the correct assumption with regards to how the speed attained by Three Socks was produced, although unable to put his theory to the test. "Anyways, we'll soon know."

"Sure and there's no way we can stop it," the postmaster replied. "Hey, though. Are Brick Shatterhouse and Moe Broody here?"

"No," Staines answered. "I looked for them 'specially. They weren't here when I arrived and didn't come with Lil Joey and the Prince."

"I'd give plenty to see their faces," Williams declared. "But I don't reckon we will. Not afore whichever of 'em it was's lost the mark young Orville put on him."

"Did you get the letter off to Ole Devil?" Staines asked, after the race had been run with the result he and his companion anticipated.

"Sure," Williams drawled, listening to the curses of the men who had bet on Three Socks and seen Black Prince cross the finish line first. "Way young Parry was going through the mail bag, I reckon Bull figured I might. Only the letter wasn't in the bag. I slipped it to Lou Temple without him seeing."

"Lou'll see it gets there all right," Staines declared, knowing the man in question to be a trusted friend as well as the driver of the north-bound stagecoach. "Let's hope Ole Devil sends Cap'n Fog and the rest of the floating outfit."

"I'll bet he does," the postmaster answered. "And, when they get here, we'll see just how big and tough the Bull's hard-cases are, by god!"

CHAPTER EIGHT

We're a Disappointment to You

"Are you Mr. Samuel Williams, sir?" asked the young man who—accompanied by a woman of about the same age—had alighted from the west-bound stagecoach, his drawling voice that of a well educated Texan.

"That's me," the post master affirmed. "What can I do for you?"

"My name's Edward Silverstone, sir," the young man replied, setting down the two carpetbags which he had brought from the stagecoach and indicating his companion. "This is my wife, Elizabeth. We heard tell you could help us get taken on as schoolteachers."

It was Saturday of the third week following the murder of Orville Webster.

On his next visit to Grattan, Lou Temple, had assured Williams that the letter entrusted to him was on its way to Ole Devil Hardin. As yet, there had been no response. Not that the elderly postmaster had expected a written answer, having warned Ole Devil that this might fall into the wrong hands before it reached him. However, he had expected that assistance would be forthcoming. Perhaps Dusty Fog would not come personally, but he had felt sure other members of the

OD Connected ranch's celebrated floating outfit would be sent to supply it.

The result of the quarter horse race had been so close that, no suspicions fell on Daniel "Bull" Keleney apart from those harboured by Williams and Walter "Trader" Staines. Even the people who had been induced to lay wagers listening to Ezekiel Barnesley were convinced that the defeat of Three Socks was no more than a misfortune. The man pretending to be the owner of the bay was a stranger to Dale County and had been vociferous in announcing how much money he had lost. As he had been seen making large "bets" with various of the gamblers acting as bookmakers, those members of the crowd who were unaware of the previous day's "trial" believed his story. In fact, he had acted so well, he received much completely undeserved sympathy.

As was the case after the wrestling match, so well had the town boss arranged everything that the postmaster and the owner of the livery barn had not made their suspicions public. None of the other events had been tampered with, being of a nature which precluded extensive gambling. What was more, by laying on a plentiful meal to follow the quarter horse race, Keleney had retained the good will of his victims. He had been so successful in this that the two dissidents realized that for them to make accusations which could not be proven would do them more harm than good. Under the circumstances, it would have seemed they were trying to absolve Staines of the blame for supplying information which was incorrect with an attempt to discredit the town boss. Should they call upon the clerk for verification, they felt sure he would deny having attended any "trial" and claim he too had been taken in by the owner of the livery barn. Nobody had seen them together, so there would be no way of proving he was lying.

Not unexpectedly, considering who was in charge of the investigation, there had been no further developments in the murder of the young schoolteacher. Using the heavy shower of rain the previous night as an excuse, he had not even taken out the posse. With thoughts of the events due to take place later in the day, none of the volunteers had objected when he gave his reasons for cancelling the search for the tracks left by the killers. Having been telegraphed by Williams, Webster's parents had sent a reply authorizing him to arrange the funeral as they could not reach Grattan in time to attend to the matter personally. This had been done and there the affair appeared to have come to a dead end.

Having been absent for a week, Brick Shatterhouse and Moses Broody returned from their banishment on the ranch owned by Keleney. Fortunately for the former, his nose had not been broken and he no longer showed signs of injury responsible for the bloodstains in the living quarters at the schoolhouse. Following their orders, they had ensured that Williams and Staines saw neither with a Winchester Model of 1873 rifle. Having left the weapon with which he had murdered Webster at the ranch, Broody had displayed an ancient Spencer carbine.

With each succeeding day, despite having learned the wisdom of patience over the years, Williams had grown less hopeful as nobody came and announced they were from the OD Connected ranch. He told himself that it was possible there were no members of Ole Devil's floating outfit at the spread. From all he had heard of them, there were likely to have been other calls for their services. The thought depressed him. Having raised his hopes—and those of his long standing friend, Trader Staines—he could not regard with equanimity the possibility of having them dashed.

Even the only bright spot to emerge as the days went by had had its darker side!

Terry Parry still checked all the mail which came into the post office and examined the duplicate forms of any telegraph messages arriving when he was absent!

The continued scrutiny implied that Keleney had not lost his concern over the possibility of outside help, particularly from Ole Devil Hardin, being summoned!

However, when it became obvious none was forthcoming, the postmaster would have lost one of the factors which had hitherto protected him against reprisals or removal at the instigation of the town boss!

The arrival of the west-bound stage had been pretty much as Williams had expected. Although he felt sure the men he was hoping would be sent form the OD Connected would not be traveling in such a fashion, habit had caused him to be present when it pulled in. There was, he told himself, a chance that its driver was the bearer of a message—either written or verbal—from Ole Devil to be delivered directly into his hands. However, he had received no indication that such was the case.

Showing that the surveillance was being maintained, Terry Parry had grabbed the mail bags and disappeared into the post office. Acting on the assumption that age and rank had their privileges, Williams had remained on the porch outside the depot section of the building. Such was his eagerness to watch for a sign from the driver, and his increased state of depression when none was received, that apart from noticing they were strangers, he had given the disembarking passengers no more than a passing glance.

Nor, from appearances, did either warrant any greater attention.

Not more than five foot six in height, the man had dusty blond hair brushed straight back. While his tanned face was good looking, it could not be termed handsome or particularly eye-catching. He had on a wide brimmed, round topped, black "wide-awake" hat, a brown three piece suit, a white shirt with an attached soft collar and plain black cravat, and low heeled brown town boots. The most unusual thing about him, for Texas at that period, was his apparent lack of armament. Certainly he was not wearing a revolver anywhere it could be seen.

Some four inches shorter than the man she was accompanying, the woman was only marginally more impressive. Although undoubtedly beautiful and tanned in a way suggesting she spent much time out of doors, she detracted from her looks by wearing spectacles with plain metal rims and having her black hair taken back, beneath an unadorned white "spoon" bonnet, in a tight and unflattering bun. The severely cut black day skirt and matching coat did nothing to enhance her figure. Rather the opposite, in fact. While even a "good" woman could wear a "Garibaldi" shirt coloured red with black braiding and buttons and not arouse doubts about her morals, the one she had on was plain white and the scarf tucked into its narrow collar was the same sombre hue as the dress. She had on black cotton gloves and was carrying a rolled parasol and reticule no more gaily coloured than the rest of the ensemble.

"I hope that the post hasn't been filled yet, sir," the young woman went on, her voice indicating she had a similar social background to that of her husband.

"It hasn't been," Williams admitted, straightening up from the porch support against which he was leaning and looking from one to the other of the couple with less perception than would have been the case in normal conditions. Doubting if either of them would be able to control the pupils, he went on, "I'm on the 'School Board,' I'll admit, but I don't have all that much to say about who gets hired."

"Well now," the man drawled. "Seeing's how you and he rode in the same outfit all through the war with Mexico, my uncle thought you'd maybe make *sure* we were taken on."

"Your uncle?" the postmaster queried, thinking how it was consistent with his general bad luck that an old Army friend would be seeking a favour at such an inopportune moment.

"Why sure," the small Texan replied, extending his right forefinger and making marks in the dust which adhered to the support of the porch. "He allowed you were real good friends in those days."

Although the gesture had seemed to be made as a result of embarrassment at having to seek a favour through nepotism, Williams could not prevent himself from glancing at the post. As he was returning his gaze to the young couple, the realization of what he had seen struck him. Hardly able to believe the supposition was correct, he looked again and stiffened like a bird-dog pointing at a covey of bobwhite quail.

The sight was exactly as the brain of the postmaster had subconsciously registered!

Two capital letters, an O and a D, were inscribed in the dust!

The straight bar of the D was touching the O!

The selection of those two particular letters *could* be no more than a coincidence!

The same applied to the way in which they were positioned!

However, appreciating what was implied by the O and D positioned in such a fashion when they were branded on the rump of a horse or on cattle, Williams was dumbfounded. He could do nothing more constructive for several seconds than stand with his mouth hanging open.

Not until the small Texan obliterated the letters, in a far from embarrassed looking gesture, was the spell broken!

"*O!—O!*" the postmaster gasped, retaining just sufficient of his usual self control to hold down his voice. "*OD Connected!*"

"That's how the brand reads," confirmed the masculine newcomer with a smile.

"*OD Connected!*" Williams repeated, showing less enthusiasm and pleasure than he had expected would be the case as he considered the implications of the confirmation. "Did Ole Devil send *you?*"

"Was I a rich, proud and haughty, Southern Belle, sir," the young woman remarked, her tone and manner friendly, although suggesting she qualified for at least part of the description, "I'd take the notion that we're a disappointment to you."

"Uncle Devil said to tell you he's real sorry he couldn't spare any more men," the small Texan went on, showing just as little annoyance at the lack of enthusiasm with which the postmaster had posed his question. "Your letter caught us at a bad time. I'd had to send off Mark, Lon, Cousin Red and Waco on other chores before it reached us. I'd've been here sooner, but we had a bunch of horses coming in for the *remuda* and I wanted to look them over myself before taking them."

Feeling as if he was in the middle of a far from funny dream, Williams thought about the names quoted to him and the way in which they had been mentioned.

The impression given by the newcomer was that, not only did he consider it incumbent upon him personally to ensure only horses suitable for the *remuda* of the OD Connected were acquired, but he had given orders to Ole Devil Hardin's already legendary floating outfit.

Such an idea was preposterous!

No small, insignificant man in dude's clothing, who did not even wear a gun, could command obedience from members of that elite group even if he was, by his own account, one of Ole Devil's nephews!

"Mark" was Mark Counter, six foot three of bone tough

fighting man, right bower[1] to Dusty Fog himself.

"Lon" was the Ysabel Kid, one quarter Comanche, scou for the floating outfit and as deadly as any member of th proud warrior race from which his mother originated.

"Cousin Red" was Charles William Henry Blaze, with temper as fiery as the hair which gave him his nickname and penchant for becoming involved in any trouble taking place ir his vicinity.

While Waco—the only name by which he was known— was not quite so prominent as the others, since he had become connected with them, he had proved himself worthy o belonging to such an illustrious association.

Not one of them, even the last and youngest of the four would accept orders or act upon the instructions of so smal and unimpressive a person.

Suddenly Williams realized the newcomer had mentioned only four of the names most connected with Ole Devil's float ing outfit![2]

The most important had been omitted!

The omission was that of the man who *led* the floating outfit!

Ole Devil Hardin's *segundo* and a legend in his young life time!

That man would *never*—!

For the first time since the conversation had commenced the postmaster looked carefully at the newcomer. He realize that he had been in error by dismissing the other as diminutiv and unimportant.

Small the young man undoubtedly was, but there wa intelligence and strength of will in his features if one took th time to look closely. Nor did his lack of height indicate he wa puny. Although his clothing tended to hide rather than exhibi the fact, there was a spread to his shoulders and a trimming a

1 *"Right bower": a colloquialism for a second in command, derive from the name given to the second highest trump in the game of euchre J.T.E.*

2 *Details of the careers and special qualifications of Mark Counter the Ysabel Kid—who stars in some of the volumes of the* Civil War serie *—Charles William Henry "Red" Blaze and Waco—who also "stars" i his own series—respectively can be found in the* Floating Outfit series J.T.E.*

his middle which suggested he possessed much greater strength than was usual for one of his size.

All in all, on being subjected to closer scrutiny, the newcomer proved to be anything except a town dwelling dude who did not appear to be packing a gun!

"Great day in the morning!" the postmaster gasped, at the conclusion of his study and summations. "Y—You're—!"

"Dusty Fog," the young woman finished for Williams as his words trailed away. "Disappointing, isn't it?"

"Y—N —!" the postmaster spluttered, for once at a loss for words. Trying to gloss over his confusion, he swung his gaze to the speaker. "I didn't know's Cap'n Fog was married, ma'am?"

"He's *not*," replied "Elizabeth Silverstone," smiling at the elderly man's obvious confusion and yet not in a condescending or derisive way. "And I pity Freddie Woods when she finally gets him."[3]

"Land's sakes, Cousin Betty," protested the young man who had introduced himself as "Edward Silverstone," but was in reality Dustine Edward Marsden "Dusty" Fog. "I make a better husband than Cousin Red."

"That's like saying anthrax is better than bubonic plague," Elizabeth "Betty" Hardin asserted, thinking of the occasion when circumstances had required her to pose as the wife of Red Blaze.[4] Darting a pointed glance towards the open door of the post office, she went on in a more serious manner, "I suppose we're all right standing out here talking together like this?"

Given a clue that all was far from being as it seemed with the newcomers, Williams took the time to subject the young woman to a closer examination than previously. As was the case with her cousin, her outwards appearance was deceptive. There was an equal suggestion of an inborn power to command respect and intelligence beyond average about her beautiful face. What was more, at that moment she was comporting herself with the assured composure of one who

3 *Information regarding Lady Winifred Amelia "Freddie Woods" Besgrove-Woodstole, future wife of Captain Dustine Edward Marsden "Dusty" Fog is given in Footnote 18 of the* APPENDIX. *J.T.E.*

4 *Told in:* McGRAW's INHERITANCE. *J.T.E.*

was undeniably descended from General Jackson Baines "Ole Devil" Hardin.[5] Yet, for all that she was said to be the grand-daughter of a man with prominence in the affairs of the Lone Star State, there was nothing arrogant or snobbish about her. Rather her demeanour was of competent, yet—unless the need to change it for something more positive arose—unassertive self confidence.[6]

Following the direction in which Betty was looking, Williams decided a correct conclusion had been drawn from the contents of his letter. While he had not mentioned his assistant by name, both she and her cousin were alert to the possibility of becoming objects of interest to Parry.

Before any more could be said upon the subject, the man in question came out of the post office. Tall, well-built, good-looking in a sullen and fleshy-faced way, he was in his mid-twenties. Like the town marshal, he dressed in a style which indicated he was not solely reliant upon his salary. There was a touch of arrogance about him as, hitching up the gunbelt with a Colt Civilian Model Peacemaker in its fast draw holster, he strolled along the porch.

"I've opened up the mail bags, Sam," Parry announced, his bearing suggesting he had done a favour rather than performed a routine duty. His accent was North Texan.

"Bueno," the postmaster replied. Concealing the increasing irritation he felt towards the assistant he had had foisted upon him, he continued in what appeared to be a casually innocent manner, "Is there anything for me?"

"Not that I've come across so far," Parry admitted, glancing at the newcomers and clearly dismissing them as nobody of importance. "But it's not all sorted yet. Don't worry, though, I can manage it. There's no need for you to come. If there is anything for you, I'll put it aside."

"Gracias," Williams drawled, with a trace of sarcasm discernible to Betty and Dusty, although it escaped the man at whom it was directed. "It's a real pleasure and comfort for an

5 *Some information regarding the relationship between Elizabeth "Betty" and General Jackson Baines "Ole Devil" Hardin, C.S.A., can be found in Footnote 24 of the* APPENDIX. *J.T.E.*

6 *One occasion when Betty Hardin found need to assert herself is described in: Part Two, "The Quartet,"* THE HALF BREED. *J.T.E.*

old timer like me to have a smart young feller like Mr. Parry
here around, Mr. and Mrs. Silverstone."

"I can see how it would be," the small Texan admitted,
with the manner of one who wished to convey an impression
of far greater worldliness than he possessed. "Can't you, Elizabeth?"

"I certainly *can*, Edward," the young woman confirmed,
but in a voice far less amiably authoritative than she had
employed while addressing her cousin and Williams prior to
the arrival of the assistant. Turning her gaze to the postmaster,
she went on, "Are you expecting a letter of importance, sir?"

"Nope," Williams denied, just a shade too quickly as if
wishing to avoid any suggestion that he might be. "Man gets
to my time of life, ma'am, 'bout the only letters he gets're to
do with his business and *they're* not a heap of pleasure."

"So that's him, huh?" Dusty inquired, having watched
Parry return to the post office.

"That's *him*," Williams agreed, stepping from the porch
and reaching to take hold of the handles of the carpetbags.
"Come on inside and let's talk this out. We'll be safe enough.
He'll be too busy going through the mail looking for any letters that might've come to do any listening to us."

"Besides which," Dusty went on, "he doesn't think we're
worth bothering about. Let me take them."

"I'll do it," the postmaster replied.

While speaking, Williams began to lift the bags. Remembering the ease with which the small Texan had carried them
from the stagecoach, their weight took him by surprise. The
discovery confirmed the summation he had drawn when
studying his visitor more carefully. No matter that Captain
Dusty Fog was built a mite close to the ground, he must be
packed with solid muscle to be able to tote such a burden with
so little discernible effort.

"We've a trunk in the boot of the stage," Betty remarked,
as the postmaster allowed her cousin to take one of the bags.

"I'll have somebody tote it in for you," Williams promised.
"Damned if this *one* carpetbag's not enough for me."

CHAPTER NINE

You're Better Off Than Me

**RULES FOR TEACHERS
PUBLIC SCHOOL, GRATTAN
DALE COUNTY
TEXAS**

Code Of Conduct For Schoolmasters:
1. *Teachers will each day fill lamps, clean chimneys.*
2. *Each teacher will bring a bucket of water and scuttle of coal for the day's session.*
3. *Make all your pens carefully. You may whittle nibs to individual tastes of the pupils.*
4. *Men teachers may take one evening each week for courting purposes, or two evenings a week if they go to church regularly.*
5. *After ten hours in school, the teacher may spend the remaining time reading the Bible, or other good books.*
6. *Every teacher should lay aside from each pay a goodly sum of his earnings for his benefit during his declining years so he will not be a burden on society.*
7. *Any teacher who smokes, uses liquor in any form, frequents pool or public halls, or gets shaved in a barber shop will give good reason to suspect his worth, intention, integrity and honesty.*
8. *The teacher who performs his labor faithfully and without fault for five years will be given an increase of twenty-five cents per week in his pay, providing the Board of Education approves.*

Code Of Conduct For Schoolmistresses.
 1. *Women teachers who marry or engage in unseemly conduct will be dismissed.*
 2. *You are not to keep company with men.*
 3. *You must be home between the hours of 8 p.m. and 6 a.m., unless attending a school function.*
 4. *You may not travel beyond the city limits unless you have permission from the Chairman of the Board of Education.*
 5. *You may not ride in a carriage or other conveyance with any man unless he is your father or brother.*
 6. *You may not smoke cigarettes.*
 7. *You may not dress in bright colors.[1]*
 8. *You may under no circumstances dye your hair.*
 9. *You must wear at least two petticoats.*
10. *Your dresses must not be shorter than an inch below the ankle.*
11. *To keep the schoolhouse neat and clean, you must: sweep the floor at least once daily; scrub the floor at least once a week with hot, soapy water; clean the blackboards at least once a day; and start the fire at 7 a.m. in inclement weather so the classroom will be warm by 8 a.m.*

"Darn it!" Dusty Fog said with a grin, after reading the notice pinned to the inside of the front door. "There's nothing I like more than getting shaved in a barber shop."

"You're better off than me," Betty Hardin replied, having conducted a similar study of the rules for the teachers employed by the Board of Education to instil learning among the children of Grattan. "I've always wanted to dye my hair and engage in unseemly conduct."

"Way you act back to home," the small Texan declared, eyeing his cousin sardonically, "I reckon the boys would say you're always engaging in unseemly conduct."

"They'd think that of *anybody* who *suggested* they behave in a gentlemanly fashion," Betty claimed primly.

"I've never known you *suggest* anything," Dusty stated. "You always tell us straight out what you want doing."

"I think I prefer being 'married' to Cousin Red," Betty

1 *We have used the American spelling for "labour" and "colours."*
J.T.E.

countered. "Of course, he's had Sue to house-train him."[2] Becoming more sober, she glanced around and went on, "Does the 'School Board' really expect us to follow *all* these rules?"

"Not according to Sam," Dusty replied. "But they could surely offer a heap of ways for firing a schoolteacher, should it be needed. Like he told us, though, Keleney didn't make use of them to get rid of Orville Webster because he'd got so popular with the parents. Anyways, I'd best go ring the bell. We don't want to be late the first morning on the job."

The time was shortly before eight o'clock on Monday morning and the two representatives of General Jackson Baines "Ole Devil" Hardin were about to embark upon the first stage of the task which had brought them to Grattan.

Taking his visitors into the living quarters at the rear of the combined post office and depot for the overland Stage Company, Samuel Williams had left them there until he was satisfied they could converse without being overheard. He had reiterated his belief that Terry Parry would be content with merely checking he had not received letters from Ole Devil or other potential sources of assistance, but considered there was nothing to be gained by taking unnecessary chances. Being in accord with his point of view, they had raised no objections. Such was the unflattering opinion of them formed by the treacherous assistant, whose appointment by the postal authorities at Austin came about through the instigation of Daniel "Bull" Keleney, that he had not shown the slightest interest in them. Waiting until he had finished for the day and had left the premises, without being aware that they were still there, they had learned the full extent of the task which lay ahead of them. Nothing they were told had caused them to believe they were faced with a sinecure. Nor had they expected they would be.

2 *How Charles William Henry "Red" Blaze came to meet and marry Sue Ortega is told in:* WAGONS TO BACKSIGHT. *Our recent researches have suggested the events took place somewhat later than we were led to assume when preparing the manuscript for publication in 1964. However, to avoid confusion, we are leaving this volume in its present position on the list of titles in chronological order. J.T.E.*

Going to greater lengths than had been possible in the letter, Williams had told his visitors of the way in which Keleney ruled the town. On mentioning the wrestling, he had learned that without ever having seen such a contest, Dusty matched his own summation of how the result had been brought about.[3] Instead of giving details of how he reached his conclusions, the small Texan had asked about the other betting coups. On hearing what had happened in the latest quarter horse race, he had suggested the same trickery as had Walter "Trader" Staines with regards to the "trial."

Listening to the questions put to him and comments made by the two visitors, the postmaster had lost his few remaining qualms and had become impressed. It had soon become obvious how the small Texan had acquired his reputation as a leader of fighting men. Nor had Betty proved any less perceptive. For all that, Williams had been concerned over the danger in which he was placing them. While Dusty was an exceptionally competent gun fighter, he was not wearing any firearms. He had brought some with him, concealed in the trunk which had been carried in the boot of the stagecoach, but would find it difficult to account for wearing them while posing as a harmless dude schoolteacher.

Learning that the "School Board"—as William always referred to the more grandiloquently named Board of Education—would be meeting on Sunday, Dusty had suggested no mention should be made of the ostensible reason for Betty and he being in Grattan before then. He had accepted the assurance of the postmaster that they would be accepted for the positions and his confidence had been justified by events.

Taking his visitors before the other members of the "School Board" when it assembled, the postmaster had introduced them as "Elizabeth and Edward Silverstone" and claimed, truthfully if without going into details, that the latter was related to an old friend to whom he owed a favour. Having failed to attract any other candidates for the post and being

3 *The events upon which Dusty Fog based his summation are told in:* THE TROUBLE BUSTERS. *However, the wrestling bout described in* Part Four, "May's Try," THE TOWN TAMERS, *occurred later in his career than the episode being recorded in this volume. J.T.E.*

under pressure from the irate mothers of the town to fill it as quickly as possible, the majority of the Board had needed no persuasion to agree. Such was their eagerness, they had asked for neither references from past employers nor any other proof of the couple's ability to perform the required scholastic duties.

Even the one member of the Board who Williams had warned might be the most difficult to convince had raised no objections to the appointments.

Studying the small Texan, Keleney had fallen into the error of many others before him—including, at first, the postmaster—by failing to look beyond external appearances. Believing the diminutive "Silverstones" would be unable to control the pupils, particularly the Bollinger twins and their younger brother, he had not felt in any way threatened by their presence. However, if he had objected, Williams had intended to pretend an inspector of schools was to make a visit in the near future. Having no wish to attract adverse attention, the "information" would lessen the chance of the town boss refusing to let them be employed. There was also, the postmaster had declared when outlining his plan to deal with the latter contingency, the added benefit that Keleney might refrain from taking any hostile action against them as a result of believing such an inspection was pending.

Moving into the living quarters of the schoolhouse, after having spent Saturday night at the town's only hotel, the girl and her cousin had employed most of Sunday settling in. As well as conveying the impression that they intended to stay for an extensive period, Dusty's primary concern had been to prevent it becoming known he was in possession of weapons. With the assistance of Williams, he had made a place of concealment under the floorboards beneath the bed. Then he had wrapped his bone handled Colt Civilian Model Peacemakers, well designed gunbelt and ammunition in a piece of waterproof tarpaulin and placed them in the cavity.

With the Colts and their accoutrements safely hidden from prying eyes, the small Texan had reassured the still worried postmaster by showing him that he had another weapon more readily accessible and the means to carry it upon his person should the need arise. The secondary armament consisted of a British-made, .455 calibre, Webley Royal Irish Constabulary revolver[4]—with a double action mechanism and a barrel only two inches in length—and an open fronted, spring retention shoulder holster in which it could be carried less conspicuously than his more usual handguns.

All the preparations had been completed!

Betty and Dusty were established in the kind of positions which they considered would offer the best opportunity for them to achieve their purpose!

The next task was to win over the pupils!

Then, if a rapport similar to that attained by the murdered schoolteacher was achieved and the wrath of the town boss incurred, the couple would use themselves as bait for a trap!

Should the lure be taken, all that remained was for the small Texan and his cousin to ensure they were the setters and not the prey!

Strolling around the edge of the room towards the rope attached to the bell on the roof of the schoolhouse, Dusty glanced through a window. What he saw brought him to a halt and he called for Betty to join him. The blacksmith shop owned by Bollinger was situated about a hundred yards away and the activity taking place behind the forge had attracted his attention.

Clad as she had been when wrestling with "Countess" Tanya Bulganin at the Bull's Head Saloon, Maggie was indulging in practice with her husband on a square of padded canvas. They were being watched by their children, two boys and a girl obviously a twin of the elder, all of whom had inherited their parents' size and bulk.

"What do you reckon?" Dusty inquired.

"She's not bad," Betty answered, speaking with authority, as she watched the buxom woman escape from a kneeling three-quarter nelson hold being applied by Bollinger. "But she's not up against a professional wrestler who'll be going all out to win."

"A few of Tommy's tricks might help her when she is, though," the small Texan remarked, showing no surprise that

---

4 *Another occasion when Dustine Edward Marsden "Dusty" Fog made use of the concealability offered by the Webley Royal Irish Constabulary revolver and shoulder holster is recorded in:* Part One, "Small Man From Polveroso City, Texas," OLE DEVIL'S HANDS AND FEET, They Were Called His Floating Outfit. *J.T.E.*

his cousin's reply implied a knowledge of wrestling. "Anyways, let's see to first things first, shall we?"

"I was just going to *suggest* we did that," the girl declared, donning the spectacles which were not necessary and had, in fact, only plain glass instead of lens, to add to the impression of mousey uncertainty she was employing. "Go and ring the bell."

"That sounded closer to 'unseemly behaviour' than just a suggestion," Dusty grinned and set off to carry out his interrupted task.

As word of the appointment of the new schoolteachers had been spread around the town by the members of the Board of Education, the children soon began to arrive in response to the summons of the bell.

Watching and listening to the excessively noisy way in which the older pupils in particular entered the classroom, as he was crossing to the raised desk where Betty was already standing, Dusty noticed that none of the Bollinger children were among them. Although no hint of his emotion showed, he was aware of the reason behind the rowdy arrival. It reminded him of the way in which newly joined recruits or recently hired young cowhands had frequently behaved in his presence as if they had been seeking to discover how much they could get away with. Drawing upon his experiences as a cavalry officer with the Army of the Confederate States, *segundo* of the great OD Connected ranch and a trail boss delivering herds of half wild longhorn cattle to the shipping pens of the railroad towns in Kansas,[5] he had anticipated and made preparations to cope with such a contingency.

Turning slowly as he reached the desk, the dais upon which it stood helping to emphasize his small size, Dusty made no attempt verbally to restore order. He knew that to do so until he was better acquainted would meet with little success and he believed he could produce the desired effect in a far more salutary fashion. Watched overtly by the giggling and jostling children, he removed his jacket and vest. Silence began to descend as he dropped them on the chair behind the desk and followed them with the cravat he unfastened just as unhurriedly. Showing not the slightest indication of realizing he now

5 *A description of one such delivery is recorded in:* TRAIL BOSS. *J.T.E.*

had their undivided attention, he unbuttoned and peeled off his shirt. There was no undershirt beneath it.

Gasps of astonishment arose from all the pupils as they stared at the sight revealed by the partial disrobing!

Except when he was attired in the well tailored and figure flattering uniform he had worn as a captain of the Texas Light Cavalry during the War Between The States,[6] there was something about the way in which the small Texan wore clothes which prevented his physical development from being apparent without a much closer scrutiny than he had been given by the pupils. No matter how much he paid for them, he contrived to make his garments look like they were cast-offs handed to him by somebody who was better favoured and, in this case, the suit was neither expensive nor of the best fit.

Stripped to the waist as Dusty was at that moment, however, the excellence of his build was all too apparent!

The small Texan was, in fact, a Hercules in miniature!

Although only five foot five and a half inches on his bare feet, Dusty weighed one hundred and eighty-five pounds. None of it was flabby fat. His chest was fifty inches, trimming down to a thirty inch waist set upon thighs and calves respectively twenty-six and seventeen and a half inches in circumference.

Still paying no discernible attention to the now clearly puzzled and awe-stricken children, Dusty flexed his arms—in what they took to be a casual, yet most impressive, gesture—to display the full expansion of his massive nineteen inch biceps. Having done so for a few seconds, still behaving in a deliberately nonchalant fashion, he picked up the bulky Montgomery Ward mail order catalogue which he had placed on the desk earlier that morning. He had acquired it from Samuel Williams the previous evening, remarking that it might come in handy without making any further explanation.

For all the evidence he was giving to the contrary, the small

6 *The tunic of the uniform worn by Captain Dustine Edward Marsden "Dusty" Fog was in a style made popular by Lieutenant Mark Counter, who became his close friend in later years. As it did not have the proscribed "skirt extending halfway between hip and knee," it did not conform with the* Manual of Dress Regulations *of the Army of the Confederate States. How Dusty attained his promotion to captain at seventeen years of age is told in:* YOU'RE IN COMMAND NOW, MR. FOG. *J.T.E.*

Texan might have thought he was alone in the classroom as he braced the book against his slightly bent left knee and grasped it in both hands. A quick glance informed him that while some of the pupils were watching him with open-mouthed amazement, others were exchanging bewildered glances. Waiting until he had their undivided attention, he put his scheme into operation. After straining slowly at first, he gave a sudden, twisting wrench which tore the thick catalogue into two separate pieces.

Listening to the startled exclamations from the pupils, Betty was hard put to hold down a smile. Contriving to do so, knowing it would spoil the effect, she continued to stand in a way which suggested nothing out of the ordinary had occurred as far as she was concerned. To the children, it seemed she had long since grown accustomed to seeing her "husband" behave in such a manner.

Impressive as the feat had undoubtedly been, Betty was aware that sheer strength alone had not produced the spectacular destruction.

While taking his stance, Dusty had used the heels of his hands to push the pages of the catalogue until they were slanted to the opening edge farthest away from his body. Doing so allowed him to begin his effort by tearing only a few sheets at a time. Finally, once the destruction was under way, he had applied pressure with each hand in opposite directions and, giving a sharp wrench, completed the separation.

"All right," the small Texan drawled, tossing the two portions of the catalogue to the floor with an apparently off-hand gesture and reaching for his shirt. "Suppose everybody sits down so we can get better acquainted?"

Although a wave of startled comments were being exchanged between the pupils, the quietly spoken words brought immediate silence. Watching the alacrity with which the order—and it was a command, despite the apparently gentle mode of speech—was obeyed, Betty felt sure they would be able to win the respect and liking of the children attending the school.

Once this was achieved, all the girl and the small Texan had to do was wait to find out how Keleney would react!

And be ready to counter whatever the town boss, a man with no scruples where employing violence was concerned, ordered to be carried out!

CHAPTER TEN

Have You Been Beating Up On *My* Kids?

Shortly after Dusty Fog had replaced the clothing he had divested in order to exhibit his exceptionally powerful torso and perform the feat of strength, the children of Cyrus and Maggie Bollinger arrived at the schoolhouse. Resembling their parents in size, they were black-haired and respectively fourteen and thirteen years of age, Cyrus Junior being the elder twin by about forty-five minutes, he and Jodie were bare footed and clad in old shirts—the sleeves rolled up to show well developed muscles—and patched Levi's pants. Mary-Anne, who was already buxom and curvaceous beyond her years, had on a worn gingham frock. Like her brothers, she had changed into this attire and left her shoes at home as a gesture of disrespect to the new incumbents of the school.

One glance at the trio as they entered the classroom was sufficient to inform the small Texan of their intentions. From what he had been told about them by Samuel Williams, he knew that he was facing the major threat to his authority over the other pupils. He was also aware that only by establishing a standard of discipline could he win their respect and the kind of rapport he required to incur the wrath of Daniel "Bull" Keleney.

Stamping arrogantly across the threshold, closely followed

by Mary-Anne and Jodie, Junior—as he was known—paused and looked across the classroom. Having seen their new schoolteachers from a distance the previous evening, neither he nor his siblings had been impressed. Nor, making a closer —if no more discerning—examination, did any of the trio see any reason to change their opinion. The twins matched the man in height and were somewhat heavier built. Even the "baby" of the family was almost as big. What was more, having been trained in self-defence by their father, they had become the undisputed leaders of the other pupils.

As had happened when Orville Webster arrived, being conscious of their position of authority, the three youngsters felt it incumbent upon themselves to test the mettle of the new schoolteachers. However, from what they could see as they entered, none of the trio expected it would prove of a similarly high quality as that of the popular predecessor.

"You're late," Dusty pointed out, sounding mildly critical and studying the newcomers with experienced eyes. "You should have been here a quarter of an hour ago."

"Why, teach'?" Junior challenged, remembering the response he had heard made by an entertainer one night when he had been a clandestine member of the audience at the Bull's Head Saloon. "What happened?"

A few of the pupils began to laugh, but the merriment died away as the small Texan swung his gaze in their direction. However, in spite of the evidence that they were at least wary of antagonizing him, he knew he must deal quickly with the latest challenge. If he did not, he would lose the ground he had gained by what they considered to have been an exhibition of abnormal strength.

"Very droll," Dusty said, his demeanour implying a hesitant rebuke which he felt sure would produce some further gesture of defiance. "Would you take your seats, *please*, so we can get on with the class?"

"Sure, teach'," Junior assented cockily, his manner indicating he considered he was conferring a favour. However, he was puzzled by the comparatively poor response to his witticism as he slouched in an insolent fashion along the aisle to the front of the class. "Whatever you say."

Watching Mary-Anne and Jodie strolling behind their elder brother in a similarly offensive manner, Betty needed all her strength of will to hold down a pitying smile. She remembered one occasion when Cousin Dusty and Cousin Red had behaved in much the same way to try out a new schoolteacher and felt sure the result would provide just as sharp a lesson in manners.

"Now lemme see, where shall I sit?" Junior drawled, turning his back on the "new schoolteachers" in a gesture redolent of disrespect. Walking forward, he gripped the boy seated at the nearest desk by the ear and began to twist it, continuing, "Here'll be a good place. That way, I won't miss nothing's—!"

Before the yelping victim could be compelled to rise, the words were brought to an abrupt end by a thumb and forefinger closing in a similar manner upon the ear of the speaker. They tightened with a pressure like the triggered jaws of a bear-trap taking hold. Finding himself being subjected to a twist of an even greater severity than the one he was applying, Junior yelped louder than the boy he had grasped and relinquished his grip.

"You'll be able to hear just as well some other place, *boy!*" Dusty stated, having crossed from where he had been standing alongside the raised desk so swiftly that neither of his captive's siblings nor anybody else had had an opportunity to give a warning. There was a vastly different, more commanding and menacing timbre to his voice and he went on, "So quit this fool—!"

The order was not completed!

Seeing his elder brother being subjected to such cavalier treatment, particularly at the hands of a person he considered so insignificant in appearance, Jodie displayed his family loyalty by jumping forward. Noble though the thought behind the attempt to render succour might have been, he soon had cause to regret trying to put it into effect.

Suddenly, the small and harmless looking schoolteacher no longer conveyed such an innocuous impression!

Not only did the small Texan appear to grow in a miraculous fashion, such was the strength of his will and commanding presence in circumstances of that nature, but he also moved with the speed of a striking diamondback rattlesnake!

While the results were less fatal, the movement was just as effective!

Releasing the trapped ear, Dusty swung and delivered a flat-handed slap to the side of the head which sent Jodie spinning across the room. Then, in a continuation of the attack, he reversed his direction and back-handed Junior the opposite way. Yet, swiftly and hard as he had struck each boy, the blows landed with far less force than he was capable of applying. Nor had he applied any of the much more severe and potentially dangerous methods he knew.

Like Jodie and all the Bollingers, Mary-Anne had strong feelings of loyalty towards the other members of the family. Expanding her already imposing young bosom in a startled and angry hiss, she prepared to avenge her brothers. Or, as they started to converge upon their assailant, to play her part in helping to teach him a lesson.

"Why that wouldn't be lady-like at all!" warned a gently chiding feminine voice. "And I just couldn't allow it in my classroom!"

There was, however, nothing gentle about the grip of the hand which closed upon the right arm of the girl. Swinging her head around, she found she was being grasped by the small schoolmistress. Yet there was something different about the newcomer. It went beyond her having removed and left the spectacles on the desk. No longer was there the slightest suggestion of meekness about the beautiful face. Rather it now bore an expression similar to that which came when Mary-Anne's mother was annoyed about something the family were doing wrong.

Never one to be unduly sensitive to atmosphere, the girl did not allow herself to be disturbed or frightened by the possibility that she was acting in a way which had incurred the displeasure of the new schoolmistress. Rather the opposite was the case. She was incensed by being accorded such scant respect by a person so much smaller than herself.

Giving vent to a spluttered expletive, which experience had taught her would have been painfully unwise to employ in the hearing of her mother, Mary-Anne snatched her arm free. Then, suspecting that "momma" would be anything except approving of her behaviour, she nevertheless swung her other hand with all the power she could muster. Possessing strength which would not have been to the discredit of a boy her age, she intended to employ much of it in a slap which would deter any thought of further interference by the recipient.

Despite hearing his cousin addressing the girl and the verbal response this elicited, Dusty could not spare so much as a second to look around and discover what was happening behind his back. He could guess what had occurred, but had other matters demanding his attention. Not only had the boys come to a halt without falling, they were showing no signs of ending their aggressive behaviour.

Darting a quick glance in each direction, the small Texan found Junior and Jodie were coming towards him with an equal display of determination. Thinking rapidly, he estimated their respective and combined potential. It was obvious that both were too angry to display either caution, or any wrestling techniques they might have been taught by their father.

For all that, Dusty realized that dealing with the boys would be far from a sinecure. Between them, they were close to double his weight and neither could be termed a weakling. Being aroused by the way they had been treated by him, should they be granted an opportunity, they might go further in their attack than either really intended.

Despite his summations, and accepting that attempting verbal dissuasion would be to no avail in the circumstances, the small Texan did not want to inflict serious injury upon either boy. This meant he would be restricted in the tactics he could employ. Should he inadvertently go too far in the heat of the moment, the very least that could happen would be his dismissal from the position of schoolmaster and he would lose his only excuse for remaining in Grattan. On the other hand, for the reasons he had contemplated, allowing himself to behave in an over gentle fashion might cause him to be sufficiently incapacitated so that he would be unable to perform the mission which had brought him to the town.

The problem was serious and there was little time available in which to solve it!

While Dusty was engaged upon surveying his predicament, Betty was demonstrating how capably she could take care of herself!

The slap being thrown by Mary-Anne was driven with all the power of her buxom, sturdy young body. She was considerably heavier than her intended victim, which should have made its effect even more advantageous. However, before it could achieve anything, it had to land.

This was not allowed to happen!

Stepping back a pace, Betty caused the girl's fast moving hand to pass without touching her. Carried onwards by its impetus, the thwarted blow made Mary-Anne spin around helplessly. Hoisting up her skirt to knee level, showing she was wearing black riding boots, Betty placed her right foot against the girls's rump and thrust. Sent reeling, Mary-Anne did not fall. Instead, coming up against the wall and being halted by it, she turned and dashed forward to resume her attack.

Ignoring the sounds from behind him, Dusty waited until the brothers were almost within reaching distance before taking any kind of action. However, when he moved, he proved that—although Junior and Jodie had believed this was the case—his immobility had not been caused by fear of their obvious determination to do him bodily harm. An instant before either's outstretched hands could touch him, he darted between them. Being unable to stop, they continued their inwards rush until colliding. Giving them no chance to part, or even fully appreciate what had happened, the small Texan turned upon them. Shooting out his hands with great rapidity, he caught each by the scruff of the neck. Then, applying a jerk which was too potent for them to resist, he flung them away from one another.

Being infatuated by Junior, one of the girls was alarmed at seeing him being manhandled with such apparent ease. Disregarding the fact that he and his brother were the agressors, she slipped from behind her desk and rose to dart out of the classroom shouting:

"Mr. Bollinger! Come quick! The new schoolteacher's beating up on your kids!"

As anybody who knew the burly blacksmith would be aware, such an announcement was sure to fetch him on the scene filled with a determination to protect his children!

Once again, having contrived to come to a stop while still on their feet, the brothers started to close in upon the cause of their misfortunes. Being somewhat heavier than his sibling, Junior had not been propelled so far away from their intended victim. Therefore, he had a shorter distance to cover before reaching their mutual objective. However, this proved to be far from beneficial. Throwing up his left hand deftly to deflect the inept blow being launched in his direction, Dusty countered with a far more competent uppercut to the jaw. Its recipient went backwards a couple of hurried, if involuntary, steps and sat down in too dazed a condition to contemplate any further hostilities.

Seeing his elder brother being knocked down, Jodie took what he imagined to be advantage of the situation by springing forward and enfolding the small Texan around his shoulders from behind. Even as he was trying to secure his hold, he became aware of the tremendous biceps beneath the sleeves of the other's jacket. Then his hoped-for entrapment was broken with an ease which caused him to back away in alarm, but not quite far enough. Spinning around as soon as he was free, Dusty employed tactics similar to those used by Betty against Mary-Anne. Driven across the room by a thrust to the chest from the small Texan's right foot, the younger brother landed on his hands and knees against the wall.

Nor did the female Bollinger twin fare any better than her brothers. Watching the small young woman turn to face her as she darted across the room, she remembered what had happened on her first attempt and decided to take greater care. Skidding to a halt where she could take advantage of her greater reach, she essayed a round-house swing with her now clenched right fist. It met with no greater success than the previous unproductive slap.

Catching the girl's approaching wrist on both hands, Betty snapped it upwards and, swivelling beneath it swiftly, brought it down. Although Mary-Anne had seen her father teaching "momma" a similar wrestling move and she had tried it with her brothers on more than one occasion, she was caught unawares and unable to avert the consequences. A startled and distressed wail broke from her as she felt her feet leaving the floor. Turning a half somersault, she alighted on her back. Winded by the impact of landing, but otherwise unharmed except where her dignity was concerned, she was incapable of considering further offensive action for the time being.

Glancing at his cousin to make sure she was all right, after he had dealt with Jodie, Dusty was not in the least surprised to discover this was the case. He knew she had received a similar training in the unusual, if very effective, form of unarmed combat that he had learned. Satisfied on the point, he gave his attention to other matters.

"Fun's over!" the small Texan announced, glaring with well simulated annoyance around the classroom. His words brought the excited chatter of the non-participating students to a stop and they gazed at him expectantly as he continued, "Sit down, all of you, *pronto!*"

"Whooee!" ejaculated the boy whose artistic skill had inadvertently been the cause of the previous schoolteacher's murder, after he and the other pupils obeyed the command with the alacrity called for by the word, *"pronto."* "Where'd you learn to fight that good, sir?"

"I'll tell you after we've got to know each other better *and* you've done enough work to deserve hearing about it," Dusty promised. "Like I was saying, before I was interrupted—!"

Another interruption occurred before the small Texan could conclude his comment!

Followed by his wife—whose face registered alarm—and the girl who had shouted to him, Bollinger charged rather than merely came into the classroom.

"Have you been beating up on *my* kids?" the blacksmith was thundering as he was crossing the threshold, without even waiting to ascertain the facts of the matter or who was involved.

"I wouldn't call it *that* exactly," Dusty answered, strolling along the aisle in a leisurely seeming fashion towards the big and clearly most irate man. "It was more in the way of handing them their needings."

A deathly hush had descended upon the classroom. Having started to take a liking to their new schoolteacher, which the way he had handled Junior and Jodie had done nothing to diminish, the pupils were concerned and alarmed by the latest development. They were all aware of just how protective the burly blacksmith could be where his family was concerned, although none of them would have known how to express it in those exact words, so they feared for the safety of "Mr. Silverstone." Competent as he undoubtedly had been in his dealings with the brothers, he was even more completely dwarfed by their father. What was more, Bollinger was famous throughout Grattan and Dale county for his ability at fighting.

It seemed to the children, watching with bated breath, that

nothing could save the small schoolteacher from serious difficulty and injury.

Such was the impetuosity of the entrance made by the blacksmith, he was almost within reaching distance of the speaker before the reply was completed.

However, while never the quickest of thinkers, Bollinger had already started to realize that the situation was not as he had envisaged. It was clear his children had come off worse in a fracas, but the discovery did not arouse him to the kind of fury which he would have felt in different circumstances. As his gaze came to rest upon the cause of their misfortunes, the full implications of what he was seeing struck him with sudden clarity and brought him to a halt as if he had charged headfirst into a stone wall. For almost twenty seconds, he stood staring at the small man who was confronting him as if he was unable to credit the evidence of his eyes.

"C—It's *you*, Cap—!" the bewildered blacksmith finally gasped, his massive fists opening and falling limply to his side.

" '*Silverstone*', Cy," Dusty said quietly, as the other's attempt at speech ended before any vital information could be imparted. " '*Mr*. Edward Silverstone,' *remember!*"

Although Bollinger was amazed by the discovery he had made, it had not completely robbed him of all his wits. Unlike his children, he had not seen the "new schoolteacher" until entering the building and he was unaware that they were acquaintances. During his service as a farrier with the Texas Light Cavalry, he had learned—along with every other member of that hard-riding, harder-fighting outfit—that when Captain Dusty Fog wanted, or *did not* want, something to happen, that wish had better be respected. Nor, if the various stories which were being circulated about his activities—since the meeting between the South's General Robert E. Lee and the North's General Ulysses S. Grant had brought an end to the War Between the States—were any indication, did it appear he had lost any of his habit of forcibly ensuring he had his way when necessary. Certainly there was nothing in his demeanour, which was much as the blacksmith remembered it, to suggest this might be the case.

"S—Sure, Ca—'*Mr*. Silverstone'!" Bollinger assented, making the amendment to the honorific as the small Texan stiffened slightly and stared sharply in reminder. Only just refraining from changing his habitually slouching posture into a smart military brace, he continued in tones of awe, "But, by grab, I *never* thought to run across *you* like *this!*"

"Likely," Dusty answered with a smile, holding forward his right hand. "I should ought to have dropped by before now and said, "Howdy, you-all," but Betty and I've been more than a touch busy since we hit town."

"If I'd've known you was here, I could've come and lent a hand," the blacksmith claimed, shaking hands after having wiped his own on the leg of his Levi's pants. Although he was seething with curiosity over what had caused the small Texan and "Miz Betty" to come to Grattan making out they were schoolteachers, he concluded from the insistence upon the use of the alias this was neither the time nor place to inquire. Instead, remembering what had brought him to the school-house, he glared and waved in the direction of his children. "Have these damned knob-heads of mine been making fuss for you 'n' M—your lady—Ca—Mr. Silverstone?"

Ignoring the other pupils—all of whom were watching with as great amazement as he had displayed on realizing who he was addressing, Bollinger gave his attention to each of his children in turn. They were rising and showing considerable puzzlement at the change from the kind of behaviour they had been anticipating. To their credit, however, such was their inborn and cultivated sense of sportsmanship that none of them had wanted him to avenge what they accepted was their well justified treatment at the hands of the new school-teachers.

"Nothing more, nor worse, than a mite of high spirits, Cy," Dusty interposed, before any of the discomfitured trio could say a word and rising higher in their estimation as a result of his immediate declaration. "Which I reckon they'll likely think twice before they try it around the class again."

"Yes," Bollinger grinned, thinking of other and older recipients of summary discipline inflicted at the competent hands of the *big* young former commanding officer of Company "C." "I don't reckon they will at that. What you got to say about it, Junior?"

"He hits near on's hard's you, daddy," replied the eldest of the children, touching his jaw gingerly. "Only it was our fault's he had to and he whupped us fair 'n' square."

"He sure did," Jodie seconded, as his father glanced in his direction.

"And she can wrassle near on's good's you, momma," Mary-Anne supplemented, darting a glance filled with admiration at Betty, but wishing her mother was not eyeing her bare feet and old dress in such a disapproving fashion.

"Where're your shoes?" Maggie demanded.

"Perhaps they left them at home because they knew I'd be wanting *three* volunteers to scrub the classroom floor after school's out this afternoon?" Betty suggested.

"Well yes, I reckon you've called it right," Maggie agreed, knowing there was no task so disliked by her children as scrubbing floors. "Didn't she?"

"Y—Yes, momma," Mary-Anne answered without enthusiasm and her brothers signified an equally apathetic concurrence.

"Fine," Betty declared. "Go and sit down. I'll see you get all you need this evening."

"How are you, Mrs. Bollinger?" Dusty inquired, as his cousin's order was being obeyed. "We haven't met, but I've heard a lot about you."

"I've never felt better, sir," Maggie replied, having come to the schoolhouse with the intention of preventing her husband from attacking the new incumbent if necessary. Realizing that only an exceptional man could have wrought such a change in him, she wondered who the small Texan could be. One name sprang to her mind, it being the most frequently used when he was reminiscing about his days in the Army, but she could not believe such an apparently insignificant person was Captain Dusty Fog. "I can't mind Cy ever having mentioned *you*, though, *Mr. Silverstone*."

"Why'n't you you 'n' Miz Betty come on over for supper tonight, Ca—Mr. Silverstone?" the blacksmith suggested, wanting to find out why the young couple were in town. "And, happen you're staying on here for a spell, happen you could teach Maggie some of them fancy wrestling tricks's I've seen you use."

"Why thank you for the invitation and we're honoured to accept," Betty assented, as her cousin glanced at her. "And I think that teaching Mrs. Bollinger a few of Tommy's tricks is a splendid idea, Edward. Don't you?"

"You won't get any argument from me on that, 'wife'," Dusty declared, having a suspicion of what was intended to happen the next time Maggie entered the ring. "Fact being, I'd count it a pleasure and honour to do it."

CHAPTER ELEVEN

They're Getting Too Damned *Popular*

"Mr. Keleney!" Terry Parry called, striding into the almost empty bar-room of the Bull's Head Saloon shortly after four o'clock on Thursday afternoon. Having hurried from his place of employment with what he considered to be a piece of important information, he had hoped to find the town boss alone so he could impart it without others hearing. "Can I have a word with you in private, please?"

Remembering the instructions he had given with regards to the watch kept upon the correspondence which came to Samuel Williams, Daniel "Bull" Keleney nodded assent. Thrusting back his chair and rising, he left Town Marshal Hawley Grenville and Joseph "Lil Joey" Cockburn seated at the table. Leading the way to the counter, as no customers were there, he waved aside the bartender and two saloon girls who were at it.

"What's up, Terry?" the town boss inquired.

"You'll *never* guess what I've just heard, Mr. Keleney," the young man stated, instead of giving a direct answer.

"And I'm a mite too busy right now to even make a try," Keleney declared, but his manner was reasonably amiable. "So you'd best tell me."

"There were a couple of fellers, drummers of some kind

105

they looked like, came through on the west-bound stage,"
Parry obliged, lowering his voice to a conspiratorial level and
glancing around as if wishing to ensure the information was
not being overheard by the few other occupants of the bar-
room. "They got to talking after they'd stretched their legs and
were waiting for the teams to be changed."

· "I've yet to meet a drummer who didn't get to talking," the
town boss commented, but with none of the impatience he
generally displayed when being addressed in such a fashion.
"So what made them special?"

"Well, it seems they were in Brownsville and saw the
Countess wrestle that woman who's coming here on Saturday," the young man replied, then paused once more for dra-
matic effect.

"And?" Keleney prompted, still in a surprisingly calm and
patient manner.

"And the Countess licked her real easily," Parry declared,
his demeanour suggesting he believed there was nothing more
need be said on the subject.

"So?"

"So, if that's the case, Maggie Bollinger shouldn't have
any trouble at all in beating her when they get together."

"By grab, Terry-boy, that's right!" Keleney ejaculated, as if
such a possibility had evaded him until it was pointed out.
"And it's worth *knowing!*"

"That's what I thought," Parry answered, clearly considering his opinion set the seal of approval upon the issue.

"Yes sir!" the town boss went on enthusiastically. "That *is*
worth knowing. I'll be able to win back even more than I lost
betting on the Countess!"

"I had that in mind, too," the young man claimed, having
been one of the many whose attempt was genuine in trying to
take advantage of what appeared to be a piece of remarkably
bad judgement on the part of the gamblers. "There's only one
problem that I can see."

"What'd *that* be?"

"I wasn't the only one at the depot. There were some other
fellers around and they heard what was said."

"Who are they?"

"Can you make sure they don't go blabbing it all around
the town?" Parry suggested, having supplied the names of half

a dozen citizens—including Ezekiel Barnesley—all of whom were more or less dependent upon Keleney for employment. "If they do start talking and those gamblers hear about it—!"

"Yeah!" the town boss breathed, once more giving the impression he had not envisaged the contingency, despite being irritated by his informant's habit of leaving sentences incomplete. "It'd make them cagey about laying favourable odds—favourable to *us*, that is."

"Then you'll make *sure* none of them talk out of turn?" Parry said, his words more of a statement than a question.

"I'll see what I can do," Keleney promised. "Way you came in, though, I thought Sam Williams had heard from Ole Devil Hardin at last."

"Not a word," the young man declared, a malicious grin coming to his lips and he continued, "The old bastard's face gets longer every day he asks if there's anything and I tell him there isn't."

"I reckon it would at that, him likely counting on it so much," the town boss admitted with great good humour, finding the failure of any letter to arrive a source of considerable satisfaction. "Unless you've got to go back to the depot, have a drink on me. I reckon, what you've told me, you've earned it."

"Thank you," Parry accepted, but with no excessive gratitude as he considered the news he had brought deserved a more munificent reward. "I don't have to go back. I'm through for the day."

"Then you don't need to rush off," Keleney remarked, dipping his right hand into his trousers pocket and extracting a ten dollar gold piece. "Here, put this to whatever you bet on Maggie."

"Has Sam Williams heard from Ole Devil?" Grenville inquired, as the town boss returned to the table, posing the question which was on the mind of the other man seated there.

"No," Keleney replied and saw relief come to the faces of his employees. He was not worried over the gratuity he had given to Parry, as he did not doubt it would come back to him one way or another. "And I don't reckon he's going to."

"So the old bastard was only bluffing about them being such good *amigos*, huh?" the marshal growled indignantly, thinking of all the anxiety he had suffered since the possibility had arisen of intervention by some of the exceptionally efficient young fighting men who formed the floating outfit of the OD Connected ranch.

"It's starting to look like they aren't close enough *amigos* for Ole Devil to send anybody, at any rate," the town boss conceded. "But we'll still play things slow and easy with him until I'm *sure* there's nobody coming."

"Then what was so important with him?" Grenville wanted to know, glancing contemptuously to where Parry was holding a drink and talking to the saloon girls.

"He's picking up some mighty interesting news about the gal who's going to wrestle Maggie Bollinger on Saturday night," Keleney replied. "Seems she got herself licked real easy by the Countess when they locked horns in Brownsville."

"Which being," Cockburn remarked with a broad grin, "Maggie shouldn't have no trouble taking her when you put them together."

"That's just the way it's starting to look, Joey," Keleney confirmed, then his tone grew more sombre. "Anyways, like I was saying, I don't take kind to the 'Silverstones.' They're getting too damned *popular* with the kids and their parents for my liking."

"I heard something about them having whipped the Bollinger kids on their first day at school," the jockey remarked, but his bearing suggested he could not believe this had actually happened.

"So'd I, but I'm damned if I believe it," the marshal supported, having met and not been impressed by "Edward Silverstone." "A short-growed runt like that couldn't whip the cream from a new-milked cow, much less the Bollinger kids."

"They say he did it, though," Keleney pointed out, also having heard the garbled version of the incident which was making the rounds of the town. "Seems he knows Cy Bollinger from some place, though. Which's why he didn't get chomped, whomped and stomped happen he did lay a hand on those three god-damned brats. You know what Cy's like with anybody who does that."

"He busted up a deputy I had for doing it," Grenville admitted. "But I still can't believe a short-arsed runt like that could lick even one of the Bollinger kids, much less all three of 'em."

"Size don't make a man tough," Cockburn put in, glaring savagely at the peace officer, always very touchy where anything which might imply a slur upon his lack of stature was concerned. "*I've* took the legs from under more than one *big* son-of-a-bitch's thought it did—and reckon I can *again*, should it be needed."

"Easy there, Joey," Keleney counselled in a placatory fashion, having no desire to see contention between his employees at such a time. "Hawley didn't mean anything against *you*."

"Of course I didn't," Grenville agreed, after receiving a glare from the town boss which warned him a statement of that nature was called for. Deciding a change of subject was in order, he went on, "Hell, Bull, why don't you fire them happen they're not what you want?"

"Because they *are* so god-damned *popular* is why!" Keleney snarled, having small patience with foolish or obvious questions unless he considered it advantageous for him to overlook their stupidity. "What I need is just one good reason for do—!"

The two men showed their surprise when their employer brought his angry tirade to an abrupt end!

However, Keleney's attention was directed elsewhere and he paid no attention to the pair's obvious curiosity!

Except when it was moved to a place of honour at the side of the ring for the prize fights—whether boxing or wrestling —which were a type of entertainment frequently presented by the town boss, his table was placed so it commanded a good view of the main street. Glancing out of the window while he was declaiming upon his grievance, he had seen what he believed might offer an opportunity to solve it. Accompanied by the Bollinger brothers and another of the older boys, "Edward Silverstone" had appeared at the end of the street and was approaching leisurely along the opposite sidewalk.

"Hawley, the schoolteacher's coming this way," Keleney snapped, swinging his gaze to the other occupants of his table. "Go and tell him I want to see him in here. Make it sound *friendly*, but see he *comes*. Then find yourself something to do that'll keep you out of sight for an hour or so."

"How about me, boss?" Cockburn asked as Grenville rose to leave without asking any questions as was advisable when their employer spoke in such a fashion.

"Come over to the bar with me," the town boss ordered. "From what I remember, you'd be plenty riled should a man refuse to take a drink with you on your mother's birthday."

"I'd take it most unfriendly," the jockey confirmed with a grin, deducing what was expected of him. "You want me to get the son-of-a-bitch so drunk the womenfolks won't reckon he's such a sweet and goody-good lil feller?"

"Either that, or let the kids who're with him see him eat crow rather than take one," Keleney elaborated, knowing the schoolteacher had claimed almost total abstinence on the only occasion he had been invited to visit the saloon. "One'll be as good's the other. Either way, he'll be through in this town."

"The marshal said you wanted to see me about something, Mr. Keleney," Dusty Fog announced, walking up to the town boss as he stood with the jockey at the bar of the Bull's Head Saloon. "Is it important?"

Although nothing showed in the demeanour of the small Texan, his every instinct warned a trap had been laid for him and he was ready to avoid falling into it.

Using his inborn flair for leadership and the commanding of respect, Dusty had attained just as close a rapport as had his predecessor with the boys attending the school. Nor had Betty found any greater difficulty in winning over the girls. They had been equally successful in acquiring popularity with the parents. In fact, despite the short period of their stay in Grattan, they had come close to achieving their purpose by creating a situation which was inducing Daniel "Bull" Keleney to seek ways of causing their dismissal from the posts of schoolteachers.

However, while acting as "Elizabeth and Edward Silverstone" had offered the girl and her cousin an excellent reason for being in Grattan and arousing the ire of the town boss, they had found the pose had its limitations. It had so far prevented any reconnaissance of the properties owned by Keleney, much less any searching of them for evidence. Visiting the factory on the outskirts might have been possible, but Dusty had not considered this worthwhile as there was unlikely to be anything incriminating in it. Despite concluding the small ranch a few miles away might prove more informative, he was unable to go there because of other commitments.

Much as he wanted to find out whether Three Socks was still on the premises along with Black Prince, the social life necessary to win over the parents of their pupils had so far demanded much of his free time.

There was another matter which had helped to occupy the hours when the small Texan was not teaching at the school.

Having no desire to let his and Betty's ability at unarmed combat become generally known, Dusty had insisted that the instruction they gave to Maggie Bollinger was kept a secret. As he had explained, particularly in view of the stories circulating about their handling of her children on the first day of school, the very strangeness of the methods they would be demonstrating would arouse undesirable interest and speculation.

Taking advice from Samuel Williams, who was the only other person in the town a party to the secret lessons, they had held their training sessions at a clearing in a small area of fairly dense woodland about a mile north of the outskirts. Proving a willing pupil and quick learner, Maggie had already acquired competence at a number of throws and holds which were unknown to her husband. As a result of these and suggestions given by Betty about attaining physical fitness, which were acted upon without question, she was now in far better condition to wrestle with a professional opponent than she had been when in contention against "Countess" Tanya Bulganin.

Despite having been satisfied with the progress Maggie was making, the small Texan had expressed misgiving over her competing. As she had been allowed to win the previous bout, he felt sure the intention was for her to be defeated by her next opponent. Such an ending would be sought as it was more likely to produce betting favourable to the interests of Keleney. Nor would he be content to rely purely upon the skill of Big Ann Derby, much less chance, to ensure victory. Even discounting the slight possibility that the murder of Orville Webster *might* have happened as Town Marshal Hawley Grenville claimed, nothing in the past betting coups organized by the town boss indicated he would hesitate before using foul play to acquire the result he desired.

On being warned of the danger, Maggie had asked whether running it might prove beneficial. Told by the *big* young Texan—for whom she had acquired a respect equal to that of her husband and Williams—it could help expose Keleney as a cheat, at the very least, she had stated her firm intention of going through with the bout. She was confident that, aided by the unusual nature of the techniques she had learned which gave her an element of surprise, she could defeat the other woman without needing the kind of unasked assistance which gained her the previous victory. There would be risks involved, especially when it became apparent that she was gaining the upper hand. However, she had declared her assurance that a careful watch kept by Cyrus, Captain Fog and the elderly postmaster would minimize them.

Accepting that the bout might offer an opportunity to do what had brought him to Grattan, Dusty had accepted Maggie's decision. There was, he had come to know, a much stronger reason for him to want to see Keleney brought to justice.

As a result of his improved relationship with the pupils, the small Texan had learned more than Williams was able to tell him about the murder of Webster. Coming across the illustration of the galloping horses, he had been impressed by its quality. On congratulating the artist, he had been told of the argument and how his predecessor had promised to settle it. On discovering this had taken place on the Thursday before the killing, he had drawn accurate conclusions about the cause. He had already known about the schoolteacher having been walking on the range on the day that the fake trial was being held and could guess the rest. However, he had conceded it would now be exceedingly difficult if not completely impossible—to obtain proof which would stand up in a court of law.

For all that nothing of note or anything untoward had happened since their arrival, at least as far as trouble from Keleney and his underlings was concerned, the small Texan and his cousin had not relaxed their vigilance. Aware that a watch was being kept upon them, which had entailed extra caution when going to instruct Maggie, they had not doubted their growing popularity with the pupils and parents was reported to the town boss.

Thursday had come without there having been any signs of animosity instigated by Keleney.

Until—

While on his way to a swimming hole on the Dale River,

with Cyrus Junior, Jodie, and the budding artist, Billie Crayne, Dusty had been accosted by the marshal and informed that the town boss wanted to see him in the saloon. Noticing a distinct evasiveness, yet a determination to have him comply when he had asked why he was being summoned, his suspicions were aroused.

Not that the small Texan had allowed his misgivings to deter him!

Concluding that Keleney most probably had something of an unpleasant nature in store for him, Dusty had gone to find out what it might be. Noticing that Grenville had already disappeared from sight by the time he reached the front entrance of the saloon, suggesting the departure had been hurried, he had told the boys to wait on the sidewalk and had entered the saloon.

Added to the way in which the peace officer had made himself scarce after delivering the message, something in the attitudes of Keleney and Cockburn had confirmed the suspicions harboured by Dusty as soon as he crossed the threshold. Nor did he underestimate the danger.

While neither Brick Shatterhouse nor Moses Broody were in the bar-room, the small Texan did not know if they—or some of the other hard-cases hired by Keleney—were near enough to arrive quickly if needed. What was more, the few customers present all lived in the town. They probably worked for, or depended in some way upon retaining the good will of Keleney and would be unlikely to take the part of anybody who had incurred his displeasure. On the other hand, there were probably limits to what they would be willing to overlook. Certainly they would regard cold blooded murder as being beyond the pale, even for the town boss, which suggested nothing of so severe a nature was being contemplated.

The last supposition was a slight comfort to Dusty!

Although the small Texan had removed his cravat and unfastened the neck of his shirt, he was wearing his coat. However, going swimming would entail stripping to his underpants. This had prevented him from carrying the Webley Royal Irish Constabulary revolver either in the shoulder holster or the waist band of his trousers. If anything hostile took place, he would have only his bare hand fighting techniques with which to protect himself.

Having accepted the situation, Dusty was prepared to make

the most of it as he came to a halt between Keleney and Cockburn at the conclusion of his greeting.

"Well now, if it isn't the new schoolteacher!" the jockey said loudly, before the town boss could speak, putting a suggestion of truculent drunkeness into his voice. "I've never seen *you* in here before."

"I don't frequent saloons as a rule," Dusty replied, just a trifle pompously, deciding Cockburn was either the bait or the actual trap.

"Well you've sure picked a good day to start!" the jockey asserted. "It's my mother's birthday and I'm just setting up drinks to her health. What'll *you* have?"

"Nothing, if you don't mind," Dusty refused, but in a polite tone. "I *never* drink this early in the day."

"Well I'll be 'somethinged'!" Cockburn snarled, teetering on his heels a little. "Are you saying's how you won't take a drink to my *mother's* health on her birthday?"

"N—Not this early in the day, thank you," Dusty replied and, although he had a slight advantage in height, he gave the impression of being smaller than the jockey. "I—I'm sorry but—!"

"I don't take god-damned kind to *that!*" Cockburn warned. "You'll have a 'mother-something' drink, or I'll be knowing the reason why!"

"I—I explained why I wouldn't, s—sir!" Dusty pointed out, sounding and contriving to look nervous.

"You will, by god!" the jockey declared, making little attempt to conceal the delight he was feeling over the response his words appeared to be eliciting. *"Nobody*'s going to refuse to drink my mother's health. So you'll either do it, or fill your god-damned hand!"

CHAPTER TWELVE

I'll Fire Him If He Should *Kill* You

"F—F—Fill my *hand?*" Dusty Fog repeated, with what appeared to be a complete lack of comprehension. Then he contrived to convey the impression of realizing what was implied by the words and his voice rose a shade as he went on, "Y—You mean d—draw a g—gun?"

"That's just what I mean, damn it!" confirmed Joseph "Lil Joey" Cockburn. "So which's it going to be?"

"I—I don't d—drink," the small Texan replied and, after a moment, looked relieved as if he had just seen what might offer a way out of his dangerous predicament. "And I *never* carry a gun!"

Watching the interplay between the two men, Daniel "Bull" Keleney considered the affair was going pretty much as he wanted. Certainly the "new schoolteacher" was not showing in a very good light to the three boys at the door of the Bull's Head Saloon. However, being aware that the jockey possessed a streak of cruelty and a temper which was not too well controlled, the town boss felt a warning was in order. Catching Cockburn's eye, he gave a brief yet prohibitive shake of his head.

Although Dusty seemed to be giving his whole attention to the man with whom he was speaking, he was also taking the precaution of keeping Keleney under observation via the reflection in the mirror behind the bar. Seeing the signal, he deduced correctly what it meant.

No less astute, and having had a much longer acquaintance with the town boss, Cockburn arrived at an identical conclusion to that of his intended victim. What was more, cruelty and temper notwithstanding, he had already appreciated there was a limit to how far he must go with his threatening behaviour. This was reached short of actually putting the threat into effect. If he should draw and shoot down "Edward Silverstone" after having been informed the other was unarmed, which certainly appeared to be the case, it would be classed as murder. Such a crime could not be kept a secret under the circumstances. Not only were there three boys watching with whom the schoolteacher was on very good terms, even though his cowardice might lose him their respect, other potential witnesses were also on hand. Should an investigation be made by peace officers from outside the town, Keleney might not be able to ensure every one of the onlookers refrained from supplying evidence.

Like most people, the jockey had too healthy a respect for the deterrent value of capital punishment to be willing to take a chance of making himself a possible recipient. However, he concluded there would be no need for him to go to such extreme lengths. If the way in which "Silverstone" was already responding offered any indication, he could achieve his employer's purpose without the need to pass beyond the mere threat even though it appeared he was ready and most willing, eager even, to do so.

"Bernie!" Cockburn said over his shoulder, knowing the bartender was taking everything in and, being aware of Keleney's sentiments where "Silverstone" was concerned, could be counted upon to back his play. "Get that gun of your'n from under the counter and put it 'n' a drink alongside the 'schoolma'am'!"

Receiving a nod of confirmation from his employer, the man behind the bar carried out the instructions as authorized. Grinning broadly, he lifted the Colt Civilian Model Peacemaker from where it lay on the shelf and placed it by the left elbow of the small Texan. Still showing signs of finding the situation amusing, he placed an open bottle of whiskey and an empty glass alongside the weapon.

"Not that one!" Cockburn snapped, wanting to ensure his victim became intoxicated quickly when he enforced his will. "Give him something *bigger*, so's he can drink my mother's health properly."

Once again glancing at and receiving permission by a nod from his employer, Bernie substituted the glass for a beer schooner which would hold more than double its capacity. Having done so, despite feeling certain there was no need for such a precaution, he hurriedly retreated a few paces as if wishing to remove himself from the line of fire. Then, like every other non-participating occupant of the bar-room and the boys at the door, he waited for the next development.

"You've got a choice, '*schoolma'am*'!" Cockburn stated, withdrawing a couple of steps and raising his right hand until it hovered above the holstered Peacemaker he was wearing. "Either you pick, pour and drink my mother's health, or you get to using that gun Bernie's given you."

"Are *you* going to stand by and let him *force* me to drink, Mr. Keleney?" Dusty asked, without taking the majority of his attention from the jockey. "After all, you *are* his employer."

"It's out of *my* hands, being personal between you and him, '*Mr*. Silverstone'," the town boss replied, glancing across the room to where the three boys were watching through the open front entrance to the bar-room. Feeling sure they and all the other pupils would lose their respect when the small schoolteacher took the drink, he went on, "Tell you what I will do, though. I'll fire him should he *kill* you!"

Dusty gave what sounded like a sigh of resignation!

Turning to the bar, the small Texan was conscious of the scrutiny of which he was being subjected by the boys and customers. It was on the former he devoted what attention he could spare from Cockburn and Keleney. As he picked up the bottle and glass, a glance in the mirror informed him that his action was a surprise and disappointment to Cyrus Junior, Jodie and Billie Crayne. It was also a considerable source of amusement to the town boss, the bartender and Terry Parry, who was standing beyond Cockburn, in particular.

What was more, if his expression was any indication, the jockey was finding the situation equally diverting!

Under the circumstances, Dusty was finding the reactions

of the men of greater interest than whatever thoughts his pupils might be having on his apparently craven behaviour!

If the conditions had been different, the small Texan might have believed he was no more than the victim of the kind of practical joke which Westerners frequently played upon dudes. He had, in fact, been the intended sufferer in such a prank during a visit to Dodge City.[1] However, with the state of affairs he knew to be prevalent in Grattan, he did not doubt this was unlikely to be the case. He could not believe, even if the reason for causing the challenge to be issued was genuine, that the jockey would dare to behave in such a fashion knowing he had been summoned to the saloon by Keleney. Such outrageous conduct could only happen with the authority of, and at the instigation of the town boss. Furthermore, if all Dusty had heard from Samuel Williams about Cockburn was true, his life could be in jeopardy, in spite of the warning signal given by Keleney.

Since his arrival in Grattan, the small Texan had not found the need to demonstrate the completely ambidextrous prowess with which he had been born and which he had further developed in part to divert attention from his lack of size. This trait, aided by his superbly attuned reflexes and training as a gun fighter, would allow him to scoop up and use the Colt placed by his left hand much faster than anybody present anticipated. However, he considered this was a solution only to be employed as a last resource. Shooting the jockey, then covering Keleney as a means of preventing intervention on the part of the other occupants of the bar-room was not the answer. He wanted to keep unknown his skill at handling a Colt, and such a demonstration would exhibit it all too plainly.

Having reached his conclusions, Dusty was prepared to gamble upon the one factor which was in his favour. While a version of the incident involving the Bollinger family had spread around the town, according to Williams, most people were unwilling to believe a couple so diminutive and apparently mousey as the "Silverstones" could have defeated Mary-Anne, Cyrus Junior and Jodie. Therefore, his ability at bare-handed combat was not known. Certainly its full ramifi-

1 *The incident is recorded in:* Part One, the Floating Outfit series (Dusty Fog) in "The Joke," J.T.'S HUNDREDTH. *J.T.E.*

cations were not even suspected by his tormentors, none of whom were aware that he could employ methods as effective and potentially deadly as the Colt would be if he picked it up.

Despite his summations, Dusty's training as a military tactician did not allow him to overlook the danger of the methods he was contemplating. These stemmed less from Cockburn than from some of the onlookers who would not care to see the plot going wrong. Unless he was completely mistaken, which he considered unlikely, they would not be content merely to stand by and allow the wishes of the town boss to be thwarted.

Accepting that he had no other choice if he wished his gun handling prowess to remain unsuspected, he started to pour whiskey into the glass with shaking hands. So well did he act, it appeared his frightened condition caused him to lose his grip on the bottle and the glass.

Already grinning broadly at the sight of what he believed to be an exhibition of cowardice on the part of the schoolteacher, Cockburn glanced and winked in the direction of Keleney as the pouring was commenced. Hearing the clatter as the bottle and glass reached the floor, he looked downwards. As he was doing so, his instincts as a fighter warned him that he was committing an error in tactics. Raising his eyes, he discovered that—although he would not have believed it possible—the warning was justified.

Having caused the requisite distraction, Dusty acted immediately to make the most of it. Nor, unlike the jockey, did he discount the other as a potential threat on account of small size. He soon discovered he was correct in his assumption that Cockburn would prove very dangerous. There would, in fact, be little enough time for him to take advantage of the chance he was offered.

Although the jockey had glanced downwards, his inattention was only momentary. Nor had he allowed his right hand to waver from its position of readiness. Furthermore, the speed with which he reacted to the discovery that he had been tricked indicated he was well trained in the rapid drawing of a revolver. His thumb and three fingers enfolded the hammer spur and butt respectively. However, demonstrating he was experienced in such matters, he neither cocked the weapon nor inserted the forefinger into the trigger-guard as he was raising the weapon towards the lip of the holster.[2]

Yet, rapidly as Cockburn was responding, the small Texan was moving even faster. Stepping forward, he hooked his left arm palm uppermost into the bend of the jockey's right elbow. Working in smooth conjunction, his other hand flashed to and grasped the off side shoulder as the left began to push. Then, pivoting around, he obtained an outside bar hammerlock so deftly it defied resistance.

Cockburn retained his grip on the revolver and the hold upon his arm caused it to be drawn free of the holster, but this did not prove any advantage. Rather the opposite was the case. Taken completely unawares by the change from "terrified" passiveness to very competent aggression on the part of his intended victim, he was unable to as much as think of a means to counter the way he was being treated. Applying pressure on the trapped limb in a painful fashion, his captor compelled him to bend forward. Then, although the left hand remained in position, the right released his shoulder to reach across and pluck the Colt from his weakened grasp. Even as he realized the use to which the lose weapon could be put, its butt struck him on the back of the head. For a moment, as he felt himself crumpling limply, bright lights seemed to be exploding inside his skull. After which, everything went black.

Having deduced that Cockburn was attempting to humiliate the "schoolteacher" on the instructions of the town boss, Parry had been no more than an amused onlooker. Seeing that things were clearly not going as intended, he decided there was a way in which he might further ingratiate himself with Keleney. Nor did he consider doing it would involve too great a personal risk in spite of the competence being displayed by "Silverstone." Tossing his glass on to the bar and pushing by the saloon-girls, he lunged forward with his hands reached to grab the unsuspecting "schoolteacher" from behind.

Unfortunately for the would-be sycophant, Dusty was far from being the unsuspecting victim he imagined!

Knowing that Parry was receiving payment from the town boss for spying upon the elderly postmaster, the small Texan

2 *Just how dangerous a failure to take the precaution could be is described in:* THE FAST GUN. *J.T.E.*

had been alert for possible intervention on his part. Once he had obtained his hold, he had kept watch via the mirror behind the bar so as to be ready for whatever happened.

Releasing the now unconscious and collapsing jockey as his intended attacker came towards him, Dusty bent forward at the waist. Allowing the reaching hands to pass above him, he set his balance on his right leg and snapped the left foot to the rear in a kick. His boot took Parry in the pit of the stomach and, while the speed with which it was delivered caused it to arrive at less than the full force he could attain in more favourable conditions, it sill arrived with sufficient velocity to turn the lunge into a somewhat winded and hurried retreat.

Alarmed by the disastrous way in which his employer's scheme to discredit the "new schoolteacher" was developing, the bartender stepped forward. It was his intention to retrieve the revolver he had placed on the counter and never expected to be used. Good as his idea might have appeared, putting it into practice proved a painful error and did nothing to improve the situation.

Seeing what was happening as his foot was thrusting Parry away, Dusty brought it down in a pivoting spin which allowed him to hurl the Colt taken from Cockburn across the bar. The aim was very good. Bernie jerked his hands away from his own revolver in an attempt to fend off the one which was approaching, but it was too late. Spinning through the air, its momentum increased by the impetus of the turn which had preceded it being thrown, the solidly constructed weapon, weighing two pounds, five ounces, struck him squarely on the forehead. Already having started to draw back in an involuntary reflex action, the impact destroyed his equilibrium and sent him sprawling to the floor. Badly dazed and with blood gushing from the gash opened across his brow, he was in no condition to save himself. His head came down on the unyielding wooden planks and he was rendered completely unconscious.

Gasping for breath, Parry became filled with mortification and rage as he realized his failure had been witnessed by the girls he was, in part, seeking to impress. Coming to a halt, he refused to allow himself to be deterred by seeing what had happened to the bartender. Instead, he rushed forward once more. Closing with the "new schoolteacher," he launched a wild punch which met with even less success than his previous effort.

Having made the turn in complete control of his movements, Dusty had no difficulty bringing himself to a stop ready to protect himself. Employing the same kind of skill he had shown when coping with the blow thrown at him by Cyrus Junior, he tossed up his right hand and pushed aside the fist before it could reach him. Making the most of his ambidextrous prowess, he struck back almost simultaneously. Not with his knuckles on this occasion, however. Instead he kept the left hand open and cupped slightly, the palm uppermost. Thrusting rather than punching, he rammed the base of the palm beneath his attacker's undefended chin. What was more, unlike in the classroom, he made no attempt to restrain himself.

There was, although the small Texan did not know it, a further threat developing. Engrossed in dealing with Parry, he was briefly prevented from continuing to keep the town boss under observation.

Three of the eight customers were men over whom Keleney could assert considerable authority. Attracting the attention of the tallest with a gesture, he nodded towards the counter. Realizing what was wanted, the man spoke to his companions—who were too interested in what was taking place between the "new schoolteacher" and Parry to have noticed the signal—rose and strode across the room.

Unusual though the method of attack upon Parry might appear, it proved just as effective as a punch delivered in the conventional fashion. His head was snapped back sharply, but he knew nothing of what came next and he went down so flaccidly it seemed he had suddenly been boned. Alighting supine on the floor, it was obvious to everybody else that he would not be capable of further hostilities.

"Look out, 'Mr. Ed'!" Junior yelled, having forgotten the disappointment caused by seeing the "new schoolteacher" behaving in an apparently craven fashion, and employing the name by which the small Texan was known to the pupils.

The warning came just too late!

Feeling his right shoulder grasped as the words reached his ears, Dusty could not prevent himself from being turned and shoved backwards against the bar. Having done so, his new assailant lunged with hands grabbing for the throat. Even as

they reached their objective, but before they could be tightened, he retaliated. Once again, he made no attempt to punch
in the conventional fashion. Keeping both hands flat, with the
thumbs bent across the palms, he drove them upwards. Passing between the man's arms, the fingers—extended and held
together—stabbed into the sides of the throat just below the
jaw. Experiencing a sensation similar to being jabbed by two
blunt knives, he released his hold and staggered backwards
gasping for breath. Thrusting from the counter, Dusty followed in a twisting bound to deliver a kick to the chest while
still in mid-air. Forced to retire even faster, its recipient col-
lided with one of his companions and was shoved aside to
collapse on the floor.

Coming down with his back turned to the last of the trio,
the small Texan made no attempt to swing around. Instead,
dropping forward on to his hands, he propelled both legs into
the air. Unable to halt, the man ran into the out-thrust feet and
was flung backwards with little breath in his body.

Returning his feet to the ground, Dusty saw the second
attacker was almost up to him. Throwing himself aside in a
roll, he avoided the kick directed at his ribs. He landed on his
back and the man followed with the intention of stamping on
him. Bringing up his hands, he caught and halted the descend-
ing foot before it could make contact. Retaining his hold, he
came to his feet. Although the latest assailant contrived to
keep his balance and remain erect, it proved of no benefit to
him. On rising, the small Texan gave a twisting heave to the
trapped limb which caused him to turn a somersault. Crashing
down on his back, he lost all further interest in the proceed-
ings.

Snarling breathless curses, the last of the three rushed back
into the fray. He saw the small Texan duck beneath his arm,
but was no better able to avert his fate than his companions
had been. Two powerful arms wrapped around his legs and
snapped the knees together. Before he could decide what to
do, he was bent across the broad shoulders of his intended
victim. Then he felt himself being lifted. The room appeared
to spin around as he was deposited anything but gently on the
counter. Shoved across it and liberated, he fell, and was
stunned by his landing on the floor not far from the unconscious Bernie.

Snarling in fury, the first of the trio showed he was neither incapacitated nor frightened by the apparent ease with which his companions had been put out of action. Snatching a bottle of whiskey from in front of a non-participating customer against whose table he had been pushed, he smashed it and rushed at the "new schoolteacher." Moving away from the bar, to ensure he had room to manoeuvre, Dusty watched the man commence an attack similar to delivering an uppercut thrust with a knife. Once again, he demonstrated that he knew a more than adequate counter. Using his right forearm in a downwards chopping motion, he blocked the thrust. Immediately he had done so, his left hand joined the right in clamping around the man's fist with their thumbs along the back of it. Keeping the trapped arm straight, he twisted its hand until the jagged shards of the broken bottle were pointing to the rear. Still applying the pressure, the strength of his grip causing an expression of amazement mingled with fear to come to the face of his intended assailant, he forced the other downwards. Shaking the hand to make it release the weapon as the man was compelled to sink to his knees and bend forward as if prostrating himself at the feet of a pagan idol, Dusty kicked him at the side of the jaw and ended his participation.

"Whooee!" Billie Crane whooped delightedly. "Did you see *that?*"

"I just *knew* 'Mr. Ed' wasn't scared!" Jodie declared, sharing the relief felt by the other boys at discovering the "schoolteacher," for whom they had developed such a liking and respect, was far from being the coward he had earlier appeared.

"He sure licked 'em all *easy!*" Cyrus Junior supplemented, just as excitedly. "Good for you, 'Mr. Ed'!"

The comments of the boys mingled with startled and admiring exclamations from the remaining customers and, despite their employer's demeanour showing he was anything but pleased by the way in which the incident had turned out, the saloon-girls. None of them could comprehend exactly what had happened, but the men in particular realized they had just witnessed a superlative display of bare handed fighting.

To Keleney, the feeling went beyond that of any of the onlookers. He was very impressed by, if far from enamoured of, the skill at wrestling displayed by the small Texan. However, having been close enough to see exactly how it had been done in each case, he found the felling of Parry and the breaking of the first attacker's attempt at strangling more puzzling than anything else done by the "new schoolteacher." For all his considerable experience as a fighter, he had never seen anything like the techniques which were employed.

There was justification for the mystification experienced by the town boss!

Dusty had been taught how to deliver such blows with the open hand by the man who now served as valet to his uncle, Ole Devil Hardin. Although uninformed people believed Tommy Okasi to be Chinese, as this was the only Oriental race widely known in the United States at that period of history, he was in fact a native of Japan. More than that, prior to departing from his homeland, he had been trained as a *samurai*.[3] While they were still children, wanting to give them a measure of security despite their small size, he had instructed Betty Hardin and Dusty in the unarmed combat techniques of that extremely competent fraternity of warriors.

The small Texan had been relying upon his extensive knowledge of *ju jitsu* and *karate*, neither of which had as yet been publicized to any great extent in the Western hemisphere, to supplement the element of surprise when he elected to defend himself with his bare hands. Experience had taught him that, added to his antagonists having been lulled into a state of over confidence by his apparent lack of stature, the techniques he had at his command gave him a considerable edge when in contention against larger, heavier and possibly stronger assailants.

This had once more proved to be the case!

"Like I said when I came in, *Mr.* Keleney," Dusty drawled, stepping away from the unconscious man and allowing his hands to drop to his sides as if satisfied there was no further need for him to be on the defensive. His eyes locked with those of the town boss as he was speaking and, glancing from one to each of the other intended assailants who were still in view, he went on, "Did you want to ask me something—or have I *already* answered your question?"

3 *Some information regarding Tommy Okasi and the samurai is given in:* Footnotes 22 *and* 23 *of the* APPENDIX. *J.T.E.*

CHAPTER THIRTEEN

She's Teaching *Him* to Wrestle?

"There you go, Annie-gal!" Maggie Bollinger said loudly, her bearing redolent of one who was issuing a dare she did not expect to be taken up, as she tossed to the floor the two pieces of the bulky Montgomery Ward mail-order catalogue which—using the technique she had been taught by Dusty Fog—she had just torn apart. "Seeing's how *I've* showed just how easy it is, how's about *you* letting all these fellers find out whether you can do the same?"

Clad in the attire she would wear in the ring, the woman to whom the challenge was directed was slightly smaller, lighter and older than her challenger. Good looking, with short reddish blonde hair which was a mass of tiny ringlets, her demeanour indicated she had no liking for what was said or the response elicited by the words.

"You'd save yourself a whole heap of grief if you kept your strength for tonight!" "Big" Ann Derby replied, her accent that of a Louisianan. Ignoring the loudly spoken suggestions from the onlookers that she should do so, she made no attempt to pick up the second of the thick books brought by her opponent-to-be and the purpose of which she had just discovered. Instead, trying to prevent herself from showing she was most impressed by the "feat of strength" she had witnessed, she

126

went on, "You're going to need every last lil bit of it you've got, happen *you* want to let me give these good old boys a show before I make you yell 'uncle' and run back to your wash-tub."

"Is that so, fat stuff?" Maggie countered arrogantly, behaving as she had been requested by the small Texan, and clenching her fists. "Maybe you'd like to see whether you can start making me yell 'uncle' right now?"

"Hey, easy on there, ladies!" Daniel "Bull" Keleney injected jovially, stepping between the two women and holding out his hands to keep them apart. "Let's save it for the bout this evening!"

"I can wait until then!" Ann asserted, scowling past the town boss and clearly making an effort to keep her temper under control. "If *she* shows up, that is!"

"I'll be up there in that old ring tonight, ready, willing and r'aring to go!" Maggie promised, accepting from her husband the blouse and skirt with which she had covered the revealing sleeveless scarlet satin bodice and black tights procured for her by Keleney. "And you can count on *that!*"

The exchange of acrimonious comments was taking place in the bar-room of the Bull's Head Saloon just after noon on Saturday.

Having arrived with her manager by stagecoach the previous evening, the professional woman wrestler was making the acquaintance of her challenger. They had been brought together by Keleney at a "weighing in" ceremony, although its main purpose was to titillate the appetites of the spectators who were present and ensure a capacity attendance for the bout.

Watching and listening to the woman, the town boss was deriving considerable satisfaction from the way in which their first meeting was going. He knew that all they said and did would be repeated around the town by the men who were in the bar-room. When it was announced that they had clearly taken a dislike to one another almost on sight, further interest in the bout would be aroused. What was more, Maggie's display of strength and Ann's refusal to attempt to duplicate it would produce a salutary effect upon the betting.

All in all, Keleney decided his affairs were returning to the smooth running to which he had grown accustomed and which had been disrupted by the arrival of the two "new school-teachers."

Much as the town boss had wanted to take some form of punitive action against "Edward Silverstone," following the debacle on Thursday afternoon, his instincts had warned this would be inadvisable.

There had been nobody else present who Keleney could compel to take up where the previous attackers had so ignominiously failed. Nor, having seen how poorly they had fared at the hands of the small Texan who all had considered to be a harmless and terrified victim, had he been inclined to take the chance of personally suffering a similar fate. To have launched an attack in response to the sight of his men's failure and been seen to go down in defeat would have caused him a very serious loss of face when news of it was circulated around the town. This in turn would have strengthened the resolve and position of those who were in opposition to his domination of the area.

Despite having the Colt Storekeeper Model Peacemaker in its shoulder holster, the town boss had not considered that using it would offer an acceptable solution under the circumstances. If he shot down the "new schoolteacher" who was clearly unarmed and whose courage and skill at fighting with bare hands against such heavy odds had won the approbation of the onlookers, he would be unable to prevent the matter becoming the subject of gossip. Once the news reached them, Samuel Williams and the other dissidents would act upon it. Even if the former had failed to produce assistance from Ole Devil Hardin, their information could cause a law enforcement agency such as the Texas Rangers or the office of the United States' marshal—neither of whom's jurisdiction was bounded by Grattan and Dale County—to make an investigation over which Town Marshal Hawley Grenville would not be able to exert control on behalf of Keleney.

Accepting that he could do nothing physical, the town boss had tried to achieve his purpose of belittling the "new schoolteacher" by pretending to believe the attack was not justified as Joseph "lil Joey" Cockburn was merely playing a practical joke. He had gained no support from his audience, all of whom knew the far from savoury nature of the jockey. All the customers had given at least overt support to the assertion by

"Silverstone" that he did not regard being threatened because of his refusal to break the habit of a lifetime and take a drink, or having an attempt made to draw a gun on him, as a matter of levity. Nor did he consider being attacked by several men larger than himself as a piece of good humored and harmless fun. To the accompaniment of muttered concurrence, which Keleney had known would not have been forthcoming if he had been beaten, he had stated that the marshal should be fetched to adjudicate on the matter if "anybody" thought he was wrong in having defended himself so strenuously.

One of the things which had helped the town boss attain his standing in the community was being willing to avoid going openly against public opinion. Although the term had not yet come into usage in such a context, he was conscious of the damage which could be caused to the "image" he had created as a "good sport" if he should persist in trying to place the blame for the incident upon "Silverstone." His suppositions on the subject had been given verification by the way in which the generally complaisant customers were now going against what he had made plain were his sentiments.

Wanting to avoid such an eventuality, particularly with the forthcoming wrestling bout offering an opportunity for another betting coup, Keleney had stated there was no need to involve the peace officer, and he admitted that the behaviour of the jockey was liable to be misinterpreted by a stranger. He had followed the declaration by claiming that the intervention by the other men was, in all probability, the result of their friendship and misguided loyalty to Cockburn. Promising to take them to task for their behaviour when they had recovered, and adopting an air of admiration that he was far from feeling, he had finished by praising the "new schoolteacher" for displaying such great ability at self defence.

That the affair was allowed to end on such a conciliatory note was not entirely the doing of the town boss. Knowing to do otherwise might push Keleney into a situation from which he could not back down and must therefore take some form of punitive action, Dusty Fog had refrained from challenging the explanations or insisting upon having Grenville brought into the affair.

Aware that he had the sympathy of the customers and that their description of what had taken place would be favourable to him, the small Texan had asked for his victims to be given medical attention. This had conveyed the impression that he was more concerned than Keleney over their welfare. Barely able to conceal his annoyance at having been exposed in such a fashion, the town boss had given instructions for this to be done. Then he had tried to learn more about the techniques he had seen employed during the fight, but with little success. Saying they were taught to him by a friend of the family, "Silverstone" had shown no inclination to go further into the matter. Stating he wished to be on his way, as he had promised to go swimming with some of his male pupils, he had asked why he had been summoned to the bar-room. Thinking fast, the town boss had invited him to be a guest at the ringside table on Saturday evening. He had accepted and left without offering an opportunity for the conversation to be prolonged.

Being engrossed in trying to reduce the effect of the debacle where the witnesses to it were concerned, Keleney had not realized the full implications of what had taken place until long after the departure of the small Texan. When the appreciation struck him, he found it as disturbing and puzzling as the events themselves. Not only had the way in which "Silverstone" acted on arrival implied he suspected he might be walking into a trap, but the comment he had made after felling his last assailant confirmed that this was the case. Taken in conjunction with his remarkable skill at fighting, such a response to a situation he believed could prove dangerous suggested he might be something other than an ordinary schoolteacher.

The town boss could not decide what else "Silverstone" might be!

Nor did Keleney come close to guessing the truth!

In spite of his misgivings on the subject, or rather because of them, the town boss had told his hard-cases that no action must be taken against "Silverstone" until he gave the word. He had no faith in their respective intelligence and organizing ability, so was disinclined to let any of them make an attempt upon the life of the "new schoolteacher" until he was sure this would not produce repercussions upon himself.

Putting aside thoughts of vengeance upon "Silverstone" until a more propitious moment, Keleney had turned his attention to recovering the loss of face he knew he had suffered as

a result of the debacle. He had concluded that the forthcoming
wrestling bout would be the best way to divert attention from
the incident. It was already a subject of considerable speculation among the population and he sought for ways by which
the interest might be increased.

As Terry Parry had predicted, the information divulged by
the two passengers at the depot of the Overland Stage Company had soon spread around the town. The general consensus
of opinion was that Maggie Bollinger was now in a far better
position than when engaged in her first bout against a professional opponent. Although she had only snatched victory from
"Countess" Tanya Bulganin at the last moment, she had
gained in experience. The mass of opinion considered, in the
light of the report given by the passengers, that she would
have less difficulty when opposed by a woman who had suffered an easy defeat at the hands of her victim.

Having noticed the arrogant assumption of "Big" Ann
Derby that her victory over the local "amateur" was assured,
when they met on Friday evening, Keleney had felt sure it
would not go down well with Maggie. As was proved when
they met for the "weighing in" ceremony, his summation was
correct. However, the confrontation had not gone entirely as
he required. He believed he had seen the red head and her
husband, who acted as her trainer, show consternation at the
sight of the catalogue being torn with such ease.

"I was going to make it easy on that god-damned over-
stuffed whore!" Ann asserted, after her opponent had donned
attire suitable for appearing on the street and left the bar-
room. "But now she's got me riled and I'll make her wish
she'd never been born when I get her in the ring!"

"What I know of her, she'll have the same in mind for
you," Keleney replied, having no doubt that the comment
would be repeated to Maggie and circulated around the town.
While this would increase the interest in, and attendance for,
the bout, he regarded it with mixed feelings and he went on,
"Anyways, Ann, you and Willis'd best come up to my room
for a spell."

"Sure, honey," Willis Derby agreed. "I know you don't
need to, but you might's well rest up a spell ready for
tonight."

Waving the red head and her big, over-weight and flashily

dressed husband to precede him, Keleney picked up the undamaged catalogue which Maggie had left behind. Keeping it out of sight, he accompanied them upstairs, and the spectators of the "weighing in" ceremony started to leave the barroom to spread the news of what had happened.

"All right!" the town boss said, holding out the book as soon as he and his guests were in the privacy of his living quarters. "Let me see you tear this like she did the other one."

"It doesn't mean *anything* god-damn it!" Ann claimed, after trying and failing to duplicate the feat without employing the technique which made it possible. "So she's strong, but I've been wrestling longer than she has and that'll be what counts when we lock horns."

"Sure," Derby supported. "Amos Thorne told me Tanya could have licked her easy enough and was doing so until he stopped her."

"And anything that old whore can do, so can I!" the red head declared. "You've got nothing to worry about, Bull. I'll whip her as soon as you give me the sign."

"Come in!" Keleney barked, in response to a knock on the door which prevented him from continuing the conversation.

"Boss," Brick Shatterhouse said entering, followed by the wizened, dishevelled and unshaven old man who acted as swamper for the saloon. "Rupe here's got something he wants to tell you."

"Can't it wait?" Keleney demanded, wanting to reassure himself with regards to Ann's ability to defeat Maggie.

"It's about 'Silverstone'," the hard-case replied. "And, what he's just told me, I reckoned you'd be wanting to hear it for yourself."

"Go ahead," Keleney authorized grudgingly, his manner showing he doubted whether the information would be worthwhile, but was still sufficiently interested in anything concerning the mysterious "new schoolteacher" to be willing to listen. "And don't take all day with it!"

"I was out to the woods 'long Dale Creek hunting 'possum yesterday afternoon, boss," the swamper obeyed hurriedly, yet displaying worry over the admission. "Only, it being so warm 'n' all, I crawled under some bushes to cool down a mite. Must've dropped off to sleep—"

"Get the hell on with it!" Keleney commanded.

"Sure, boss," the elderly man assented. "When I woke up, I saw Maggie Bollinger teaching the "new schoolteacher" how to wrestle."

"*She* was teaching *him* to wrestle?" the town boss spat out, too startled at the possibilities opened by the information to comment upon his employee having been absent from work without permission.

"She sure was, boss," the swamper confirmed. "When I looked out, she was letting him do a real fancy throw on her. Then she got up and showed him how to do it right."

"Who else was there?" Keleney wanted to know.

"Cy, Sam Williams and the 'new schoolma'am'," the man listed.

"So *that's* their god-damned game!" the town boss ejaculated. "Why the hell didn't you say something about it afore now?"

"I—It sort of slipped my mind," the swamper lied, alarmed by the anger his employer was displaying, although the truth was that he had hoped nobody had missed him and had had no wish to call attention to his unauthorized absence. "I only remembered when Brick asked just now where I was yesterday."

"Did they know you were watching?" Keleney demanded, guessing the real reason for the omission and being willing to overlook it in his eagerness to learn more about what the old man had seen.

"No, sir!" the swamper answered with confidence. "I figured's, seeing's they'd come out there 'stead of doing it behind the forge, they didn't want *nobody* to know what was doing and kept hid until they'd gone."

"What's up, Bull?" Derby asked, surprised by the vehemence with which the town boss was reacting to the information.

"That 'mother-something schoolteacher' knows fighting tricks the like of which I've *never* seen before!" Keleney explained and, having described the incident in the bar-room, he concluded, "If he's taught her just a few of them, she'll take Ann like Grant took Richmond!"

CHAPTER FOURTEEN

Am I Going To *Have Fun* With You?

"We've got where we're going, 'schoolma'am'," the taller of the two gun-hung hard-cases declared, closing the door of the building into which they had escorted their blindfolded and resisting prisoner. "You can haul down that bandana from over your eyes now, seeing's how you won't know where you're at. But it won't do you the teensiest mite of good to start yelling for help. 'Cepting for Milt 'n' me, there ain't *nobody* close enough to hear you and having you caterwauling'd only rile us up."

"Which same you for certain sure wouldn't take kind to us doing *that,* gentle's we've been so far, lil gal," claimed the second of the pair, his accent also that of a North Texan. "So, happen you've got right good sense, you'll keep on doing what Snackey 'n' me tells you. Then, comes around noon tomorrow, you'll be turned loose safe 'n' sound to go back to the schoolhouse."

Continuing to behave in the frightened and submissive manner she had adopted on being captured in Grattan, Betty Hardin reached up to remove the blindfold. As she did so, she told herself silently that she would soon be finding out just how good a judge of human nature she might be.

Knowing Ezekiel Barnesley had been an active participant

in more than one of the nefarious schemes of Daniel "Bull" Keleney, the girl was wary of him when he had come to the schoolhouse shortly after Dusty Fog left to attend the wrestling bout at the Bull's Head Saloon. Her suspicions were aroused when the clerk had asked if she would go to one of her female pupils who had met with an accident. Although she had not been able to leave a note informing her cousin of what had happened, she knew that to refuse to go would be out of character, and she had accompanied Barnesley to an empty house on the outskirts of the town. She had not been surprised to find there was no injured pupil in the building. Nor, despite feeling sure he did not know it was to be done, had she been persuaded that the clerk was innocent of deception when he was felled by a blow from the taller of the two men who were present.

Thinking fast, Betty had assessed the situation and reached her conclusions. The assault upon the clerk had diverted the attention of one man. However, as the other hard-case had continued to watch her, she had decided against putting to use her extensive knowledge of *ju jitsu* and *karate,* or attempting to draw the Remington Double Derringer, she had taken to carrying fastened in the top of her left riding boot. The blouse and divided skirt she had on would have permitted a greater freedom of movement than the attire she wore when acting as schoolteacher, but her study of the pair had suggested neither course was advisable. Although their clothing was that of working cowhands, she had judged them to be professional fighting men and not only with firearms. In their early forties, they had not struck her as the kind who would panic or act rashly in an emergency. Rather they had the age, intelligence and experience to respond with efficiency should the need to do so arise.

All the conclusions drawn by the girl had warned that, good as she undoubtedly was, she could not hope to render both men *hors de combat* in such quick succession to rule out the chance of failure. As soon as she had launched her attack upon the first, the second hard-case who was dealing with Barnesley would intervene before she could arm herself with the Remington. Nor would merely screaming for help have offered an acceptable solution. The area around the building had been deserted as she and the clerk were passing through it. Knowing how public sentiment regarded the molestation of a "good" woman, neither hard-case would be willing to risk being caught while engaged in something which might be construed as attacking her, and they would have had no hesitation before silencing her. While they might not go so far as shooting, unless she started to bring out the Double Derringer, a blow to the head from either's Colt would achieve their purpose just as effectively.

An awareness of the possible consequences was not the only motive Betty had had for deciding to surrender!

Pointing out that their lives might depend upon making a correct identification, Dusty had insisted Betty and he become acquainted with the appearances of the men hired by Keleney. She had not seen the pair before that day, but believed they were in his employ. Guessing what they had been ordered to do and aware that she had no other choice at that time, she had not attempted to resist. Instead she had conveyed the impression of being too frightened to do so, in the hope of verifying her suspicions and obtaining conditions more suitable for her escape.

As yet, the girl had achieved neither of her purposes. She knew that she must do something without too much more delay. Despite the facts that she had been blindfolded before she was driven away in the buggy, and that there had been no opportunity to take action during the journey, her range bred senses had formed a pretty fair estimation of how far and in which direction she had been taken. Remembering all she had learned about the geography of Dale County since her arrival, she believed she knew her present location.

All that remained to be done, Betty thought, was to acquire the information she sought with regards to the identity of the person responsible for her abduction.

And to escape from captivity as quickly as possible!

Unfastening and removing the blindfold, Betty found that Milt was lighting a lamp. Blinking a little in the glare, she glanced around. She was in a small and poorly furnished room of an adobe building, but there was nothing visible to suggest by whom it was owned.

"Go and sit down," Snackey ordered, waving a hand towards the rikety table which—along with three chairs and a couple of bunks—formed the only furnishings of the room.

"Behave yourself and, like we told you back to Grattan, you'll not get hurt."

"Don't worry, gentlemen," Betty replied in her normal voice, strolling across the room with none of her previous apparently frightened subservience. Looking at her captors in a mixture of pity and assurance as she sat down, she went on, "I've no intention of causing *any more* trouble for you, because you *could* be in more than enough already without me adding to it. In fact, I hope Bull Keleney is making what you're doing worth your while."

"*Bull Keleney?*" Milt said, trying without too much success to sound puzzled. "Well now, lil gal, we've heard tell of the Bull, natural', but what makes you think it's him's done it?"

"This is a line cabin belonging to his ranch," Betty guessed.

"How the hell did *you* know that?" Milt growled, confirming the girl's supposition.

"Just an educated guess," Betty replied. "Which you've proved is correct."

"Well you guessed wrong about it being *him's* told us to fetch you here!" Milt claimed, annoyed rather than puzzled by the way in which the captive was behaving. "Fact being, I reckon the Bull'd be right riled should he hear we brought you here."

"I'm *sure* he would," Betty conceded sardonically, keeping both hands in sight. "By the way, did—*whoever*—hired you tell you who I am?"

"You're the new schoolteacher's wife and—!" Milt began, still drawing no conclusions from the change in the girl's demeanour although his companion was studying her in a speculative fashion.

"And I'm also *Ole Devil Hardin's* granddaughter," Betty interrupted.

"Oh sure you are!" Milt scoffed, paying no attention to the startled exclamation which burst from the other hard-case. "And I'm the only son of General Robert E. Lee hisself!"

"Can I take something from my pocket?" Betty requested.

"Go to it," authorized Snackey, to whom the words were directed, throwing a prohibitive glare at Milt before he could make any further comment and causing him to close his mouth with speaking. "But be *real* careful what you bring out!"

"Here," Betty said, taking from the pocket of her divided skirt an item which she had been carrying as a precaution since reaching Grattan, and offering it to the taller of her captors.

"Well I'll be switched!" Snackey growled, his tone redolent of consternation, having identified the brand of the OD Connected ranch carved into the covers of the thin brown leather wallet he had been given. However, the main cause of his ejaculation was the tintype he had discovered was its sole contents. "Take a looked at *this*, Milt!"

"It's Ole Devil for sure, I've seen his likeness more'n once in newspapers!" the second hard-case declared, staring from the girl to the portrait of her standing alongside a stern-faced, somewhat Mephistophelian-looking elderly man who was sitting in a wheelchair, and then looked back at her.[1] "What's that writing on it say, Snack?"

"'To my grandaughter, Betty'," the taller of the abductors read. "And it's signed, 'Jackson Baines Hardin'!"

"Of course it is," the girl confirmed, exuding the calm assurance of one who believed she was in complete control of the situation and had nothing to fear. "Grandfather wasn't baptized 'Ole Devil,' you know."

"We *know* what his name is!" Milt asserted, throwing a worried look at his companion. "But Bri—We wasn't told nothing about you being *his* kin."

"Keleney doesn't know we are, or he'd never let 'Cousin Edward' and I become the schoolteachers," Betty replied truthfully, dropping the pretense of not knowing who was the instigator of the abduction. However, her veracity did not continue as she elaborated upon the explanation. "Nor does he know that the Ysabel Kid and Waco are close by, in case we should need their help."

"T—The Kid's *here?*" Milt gulped, turning a hurried and alarmed glance to the window which was mute testimony to his belief that the awesome reputation of the man in question was well deserved.

1 *How General Jackson Baines 'Ole Devil' Hardin sustained the injury which confined him to a wheelchair is told in the* "The Paint" *episode of* THE FASTEST GUN IN TEXAS. *J.T.E.*

"He is," Betty prevaricated, but with such conviction she might have been speaking the truth. "And with Waco to back him."

"So the Kid's around, huh?" Snackey said quietly, but in a suspicious fashion. "Then how come he didn't cut in when we grabbed you?"

"Because neither he nor Waco were at the school when Barnesley brought the message to me," the girl replied. "But they'll start looking for me as soon as 'Cousin Edward' tells them I'm missing. I'm sure they'll be able to—*persuade*— either Brick Shatterhouse or Moe Broody to tell them what's happened to me. The Kid, in particular, is *very* good at *persuading* people to answer questions, as I expect you know."

For all her apparent lack of concern, while speaking, Betty was watching the way in which her captors were reacting to the words!

The girl knew she would very soon be discovering how accurately she had assessed the pair's characters!

If the two hard-cases had been younger, less obviously competent, or more openly reckless in their behavior, Betty would not have allowed herself to be taken so easily. As it was, although she had not considered they would prove cowardly or stupid, she had believed the passing of the years would have taught them how to balance courage against sensible caution. She had gambled that, learning they had inadvertently abducted a person who had such influential family connections and claimed to have such potentially dangerous support in the vicinity, they would be more likely to listen to reason than if they were less experienced and, in consequence, were desirous of establishing a reputation for bravery.

"Then why'd you let us grab you?" Snackey demanded, after a brief exchange of glances with his companion which were observed with relief by the girl.

"Because you didn't *'grab'* me as such," Betty answered. "I was hoping you'd take me to Keleney, or at least to somewhere which would prove he'd hired you."

"You're either real nervy, or not over smart, lady," Snackey declared. "Happen the Bull had hired us—and I'm not saying's how it was *him* as did——he for sure wouldn't've let you get away to tell about it."

"He might not want to, but *you* would make sure he did,"

the girl claimed with assurance. "Neither of you is the kind of stupid young gun-slick trying to build a name who'd be willing to stand up against the Kid and Waco to show you dare do it. Once you heard who I am, being smart enough to work out the consequences, you'd make good and sure *nothing* happened to me."

"Now why'd we do that?" Milt challenged, but something in his manner indicated he was pleased by the complimentary conclusions in spite of being ill at ease over the discovery of the identity of their captive.

"Because *neither* of you are fools," Betty claimed, showing none of the satisfaction which was beginning to assail her. "You'd know that, even if you got away before the Kid arrived, you'd never again draw a safe breath no matter where you went. Not only would he and Cousin Dusty be after you, grandfather would put such a bounty on your heads *everybody* would be looking for a chance to collect it."

"Seems like you've got *everything* worked out pretty good, ma'am," Snackey commented. "So what've you got in mind now?"

"Tell me who hired you and you're free to go," Betty replied. "If you do that, I'll give you my word that you'll not be hunted or molested in any way."

"Brick Shatterhouse took us on and told us what to do," Snack asserted, after looking at and receiving a nod of concurrence from his companion. "I could say's how he told us the Bull gave the word for it, but *that'd* be a lie."

"Brick don't breath twice in a row without the Bull says he can, though," Milt supplemented.

"So I understand," Betty drawled. "Did he tell you why they wanted me brought out of the way for the night?"

"Allowed's how he'd got a fair sum of money bet on Big Ann and wanted to make sure Maggie Bollinger let her win," Snacked replied. "Which meant's how the Bull was backing him on it. Anyways, seeing's how we was close to the blanket and all we had to was fetch you here, then turn you loose right side up 'n' all your buttons fastened comes noon, we took the chore."

"We didn't mean you no real harm, ma'am," Milt affirmed. "No matter how rough we talked to keep you quiet."

"I never thought you *did,*" Betty claimed reassuringly. "Which's why I came along so easily."

"Mind happen I ask why a for-real lady like you come to Grattan and's taking such chances, ma'am?" Milt queried.

"Sam Williams doesn't like the way Bull Keleney runs the town and believes he was responsible for the last school-teacher being murdered," Betty explained. "But he knew he couldn't do anything, or *prove* his suspicions alone. So, as he's an old friend of grandfather, he sent to ask for help. 'Cousin Edward' and I decided the best way we could give it was to pretend we were schoolteachers and see what we could stir up."

"Who is this 'Cousin Edward,' ma'am?" Snackey inquired. "What we've heard, he's some bear-cat in a fight, but I don't recollect hearing his name afore."

"You know him better as 'Dusty Fog,'" the girl replied, having refrained from divulging the information earlier as she had considered it might reduce the effect of her explanation.

"Dusty Fog?" Milt repeated, as Betty had known would be the case when she gave her cousin's name. "But that feller in Grattan's only a short-growed runt—."

"He's still Dusty Fog," the girl stated with a smile. "I've no reason to lie to you about it."

"There's no reason at all why you should," Snackey agreed. "Anyways, we'll be going now, ma'am. Only, to make sure you don't head back to town afore we're well clear, we're going to unhitch the hoss from the buggy. You can hitch him up again as soon's you can't hear us no more."

"That's all right with me," Betty assented without a moment's hesitation. She had suspected something of the sort was behind the abduction, but was satisfied there was sufficient time for her to return to the town and remove the restriction it would place upon Maggie. "Or you can leave it hitched and I'll give my word that I'll stay in here until you're well on your way. Either's fine with me."

"We'll take your word, ma'am," Snackey decided and Milt nodded concurrence.

"Bueno," Betty declared, delighted to find her judgement was correct and, on learning her true identity, the men had behaved as she anticipated. "And don't worry. I don't hold any grudge against you. There'll be no repercussions from the OD Connected. Nor will Cousin Dusty and I tell *anybody* you've answered my questions."

"Gracias, ma'am," Snackey drawled and, knowing the

future careers of Milt and himself could be affected adversely if word was spread that they had betrayed an employer, even indirectly, his gratitude was genuine. "I'll give *you* one for that. You mind the last quarter hoss race the Bull had run, when everybody figured's how his Black Prince would get licked, but it didn't happen that way?"

"I've heard about it," the girl admitted.

"Three Socks, the hoss's was supposed to be fast enough to beat the Prince, is still out to the Bull's spread," Snackey informed. "We saw and heard about it when we dropped by to ask if he was hiring. Will that help you 'n' Cap'n Fog?"

"It certainly will!" Betty confirmed. "And, should we have to use it, we'll make sure Keleney doesn't find out *how* we learned Three Socks was there."

"*Gracias* again, ma'am!" Snackey thanked.

"You're one hell of a spunky lil g—lady, ma'am," Milt went on. "And it's been right pleasureable knowing you. *Adios*, ma'am."

Watching the door close behind the two hard-cases, Betty was well satisfied with the way in which the affair had turned out. While she could not envisage how Keleney meant to deal with the questions aroused by her abduction if it had gone as he intended, she was convinced the evidence she had acquired would make a significant contribution towards achieving the purpose which had brought her cousin and herself to Grattan. She was confident that, although the unsupported word of "Elizabeth Silverstone" might not have carried enough weight to convince the people of the town, they would be willing to give credence to the story told by the granddaughter of Ole Devil Hardin. What was more, learning that they would have the backing of Dusty Fog might stiffen their resolve and give them sufficient collective courage to make a stand against the domination of Keleney and his hard-cases.

Having given her word, the girl had no intention of leaving the building as soon as she heard Snackey and Milt riding away. That was alien to the way in which she had been raised to act. Instead, as she had promised, she remained seated at the table until her instincts suggested they were out of hearing distance.

Just as Betty was concluding that honour was satisfied and she could take her departure, the door of the cabin opened!

"What do *you* want?" the girl asked, coming to her feet.

"You, what else?" Joseph "Lil Joey" Cockburn replied, stepping across the threshold and starting to close the door behind him.

Looking past the newcomer before he completed the closure, Betty saw a horse standing ground hitched by its dangling reins. As she had not heard either hoof beats or the creaking of leather made by the rider dismounting, she deduced he must have arrived on foot and leading the animal to lessen the sounds of its approach. She did not care for the conclusions she began to draw from such a precaution having been taken.

"M—Me?" the girl gasped, with a resumption of the frightened manner she had discarded a short while earlier, being aware that she could be facing a far greater danger than had been posed by the two hard-cases.

"*You!*" Cockburn confirmed in a mocking tone, leering and strolling forward. "I don't know where those two jaspers've gone, but it saves me having to get rid of them and they'll get the blame for it."

"F—For what?" Betty inquired tremulously.

"Girlie, am I going to have *fun* with you?" the jockey warned, continuing his unhurried advance. "It's just a goddamned pity that 'mother-something husband' of your'n ain't going to live long enough to hear tell what I've done to you, though."

"W—How do you m—mean?" Betty asked, her perturbation increasing, but not entirely on her own behalf.

"He'll've got word by now that you've been took off," Cockburn explained. "And, when he does's he'll've been told, he's going to find out how that other son-of-a-bitching schoolteacher was killed!"

CHAPTER FIFTEEN

We've Got Your Wife

"Hey, 'Mr. Silverstone,'" said the attractive blonde saloon-girl who had made her way through the crowd with the deft ease of long experience, holding out a folded sheet of paper to the small Texan at the same time as—unbeknown to him—Betty Hardin was being confronted by Joseph "Lil Joey" Cockburn at the line cabin. "A feller asked me to give this to you. He said you should read it straight off, without letting *anybody* see you, and do just what it tells you to."

As Daniel "Bull" Keleney had predicted, so much interest had been aroused by the reports of the confrontation between the contestants during the "weighing in" ceremony, that the bar-room of the Bull's Head Saloon was packed to capacity.

Being unaware that the town boss had learned Dusty had been giving Maggie Bollinger instruction in wrestling, he had arrived alone. He had been met at the door by Keleney and taken to the ring-side table. After he had been introduced to Willis Derby, his polite refusal to accept a drink had allowed his host to be heavily jocular about the inadvisability of trying to force liquor upon him. The remark had caused the small Texan to look for the man whose behaviour had led to it being made. While Brick Shatterhouse and Moses Broody were hovering close by, there had been no sign of Cockburn. Yet, according to Samuel Williams, the jockey was always included among the guests at the table of the town boss. Another noticeable absentee had been Town Marshal Hawley Grenville.

Before Dusty could attempt to discover why two such prominent members of Keleney's coterie were missing, a waiter had come to the table and said that several children were outside the building, trying to look through the windows. Praising the way in which the "new schoolteacher" had won the respect of the pupils, Keleney had suggested he should deal with the situation rather than sending some of the saloon's employees to chase them away. Going outside, he had gathered the children around him. Promising he would describe the bout and demonstrate some of the throws on Monday morning, he had told them to go home. As had become the case, his orders had been obeyed without argument. Knowing there might be trouble when the bout ended with what the town boss would regard as an unfavourable decision, he had suggested that the Bollinger twins and their younger brother went to the schoolhouse and waited with "Miz Elizabeth." Returning to the bar-room after they had taken their departure, and seeing the combatants were entering the ring, he was barely across the threshold when he was intercepted by the girl.

"Where is he?" Dusty inquired, without opening the sheet of paper.

"I dunno," the blonde answered, her attention on the ring rather than the man she was addressing. "He went out of the side door as soon's he'd told me what to do 'n' say."

"Who was he?" the small Texan asked.

"I don't know. I've never seen him afore."

"What did he look like?"

"Huh?"

"Was he a cowhand, a gambler, or what?"

"He'd got on store bought clothes's all I know," the blonde declared, her bearing redolent of one who had done all that was required of her and now wanted to carry on with her own affairs. "Like I said, he was a stranger. Looks like they'll soon be starting and I want to get to some place I'll be able to watch 'em."

Concluding he was unlikely to learn anything useful from

the girl and she would only grow resentful if he continued to question her, Dusty raised no objections to her departure. As she turned and walked away, he opened the sheet of paper. Noticing that the writing was neat and completely legible, he stiffened slightly as he began to read the message.

"*Silverstone,*

We've got your wife!

If you want her back safe and uninjured, come straight to the schoolhouse. Don't try to tell Sam Williams, Cy Bollinger, or anybody else what has happened. We're having you watched and it will be the worse for her unless you do exactly as we tell you. Bring this letter with you. Come right away and, remember, her life is in your hands."

There was no signature!

Nor, after reading the first few words, had Dusty expected there would be!

Despite the intense mental turmoil which was aroused by the message, no sign of emotion showed on the tanned face of the small Texan. Folding the paper and stuffing it into the inside pocket of his jacket, he glanced around quickly in the hope of locating anybody who was clearly watching him. He failed to do so, but realized this did not prove the writer had lied about him being kept under observation. His scrutiny had, of necessity, been brief. Nor, under the circumstances, was there sufficient time for him to make a more lengthy examination of his surroundings.

For a moment, Dusty turned his gaze to the ring. Accompanied by her husband and Williams, who were to act as her seconds, Maggie was standing in the corner nearest to him. Even as he looked, the referee crossed and handed the postmaster a piece of paper identical to the one he had received from the blonde. However, he could not think of any way by which he might attract their attention without allowing it to be seen he was disobeying his instructions.

Thinking fast, the small Texan conceded there was only one course left open to him under the condition which prevailed. He did not doubt that, in some way, his cousin had been taken prisoner. Having seen that Williams had received a message which he believed to have originated from the same source as his own, he could guess why this was done. He drew some slight consolation from his note having been addressed to him by his alias, as this implied that his true identity was still unknown. Against that, however, he realized the abductors would be less likely to take extreme measures against the granddaughter of Ole Devil Hardin than they would when dealing with somebody whose influential family connections were unknown.

Competent as Dusty knew Betty to be, he was aware that he must do nothing which might make her position more precarious. He did not doubt that Keleney was behind whatever had happened to her and, concluding a showdown was likely to be forthcoming in the near future, realized he was in no position to meet it. Suspecting his display of fighting ability against Cockburn and the other attackers had aroused even more interest in himself, he had deduced he would be subjected to extra careful scrutiny on his arrival at the saloon. Wanting to avoid giving a warning that he was anticipating trouble, he had arranged for the postmaster to carry his Webley Royal Irish Constabulary revolver in the box containing the gear for ministering to Maggie between the falls. It would be available to him if he returned to the bar-room after obeying the instructions, but he considered he would require more adequate armament for the confrontation he felt sure was in the offing.

In addition to the small Texan's concern for the welfare of his cousin, there was another reason for him to avoid delaying his departure. He had told the Bollinger children to join her at the schoolhouse and did not doubt they would obey. By doing so, they might inadvertently spring the trap he believed had been laid for him.

Relying upon Williams and the Bollingers to realize he must have a *very* good reason for diverging from the arrangements he had made with them, Dusty left the building. He suspected that the abduction of his cousin had the dual purpose of luring him into an ambush and ensuring Maggie was so worried she did not beat Big Ann Derby. Although his note had made no mention of the latter, the one delivered to the postmaster could have no other purpose. In which case, being intelligent enough to guess what had caused his departure, Williams would advise her to keep the fight going as long as possible in the hope that he could effect a rescue and return.

Listening to the sounds from the saloon which indicated the

bout was under way, as he strode swiftly along the street, the small Texan wondered whether the spectators were being excessively noisy. He could guess the reason for this. Although he did not believe such a contingency would arise before he reached the schoolhouse, he took the precaution of keeping to the shadows as much as possible in case he was wrong. Despite his caution having proved needless, he did not regret employing it when he came into view of his destination without having been molested.

Much to his consternation, however, Dusty saw that Mary-Anne, Cyrus Junior and Jodie Bollinger were almost at the front door of the schoolhouse!

"For the Lord's sake stay real calm, 'specially *you*, Cy!" Samuel Williams commanded rather than advised, having read the note given to the referee by one of the saloon-girls and then brought to him. "This's real *bad* news, but we're being *watched* and, until we know more about it, we've got to do just like we're told!"

"What's up then, Sam?" Cyrus Bollinger demanded, realizing only a matter of the gravest importance would produce such a noticeable reaction from the—as far as appearances went—generally unemotional postmaster.

"Don't neither of you lose your tempers, nor try to do *nothing* hasty!" Williams warned with grim urgency, but screwing the sheet of paper into a ball as if its contents were of no interest. "Things're bad enough without making 'em worse. They've got Miz Betty—!"

"Miz Betty?" the blacksmith spat out, only just retaining sufficient presence of mind to tone down his voice. *"Who's got her?"*

"The message don't say who they be," the postmaster replied, pushing the crumpled paper into the back pocket of his trousers. "Which I reckon we can make us a pretty fair guess at who-all's behind it."

"Yeah!" the blacksmith growled, tensing.

"Steady, Cy!" Maggie Bollinger commanded, just as startled and alarmed by the news. However, she contrived to keep her feelings under control and the words served to prevent her husband from behaving in an ill-advised manner. Satisfied on this point, despite feeling sure she could guess the answer, she

went on, "What've they got her for, Sam?"

"They say for you to give the customers here a good show first," Williams replied, as the woman had anticipated. "But you've got to make good and sure's Big Ann winds up the winner."

"That's what I thought it'd be," Maggie admitted.

"We've got to let Cap'n Dusty know what's doing!" Bollinger asserted, but waited to see what the elderly postmaster considered was the best way in which the suggestion could be put into practise.

"That we have!" Williams agreed, then looked around in what appeared to be a casual fashion. Employing all his skill as a poker player to conceal his consternation, he exchanged a wave with Daniel "Bull" Keleney. Then, returning his attention to the Bollingers—who had conducted a similar scrutiny and had also noticed that the man they were seeking was absent—he continued, "Could be he *knows* already."

"Then he'll've gone to look for her!" Maggie deduced, and she received a nod of grim agreement from the elderly postmaster.

"But he don't have no gun with him!" Bollinger pointed out, glancing at the box which held revolvers for himself and Williams as well as the Webley R.I.C. belonging to Dusty Fog. "I'd best take—!"

"*No*, Cy!" the postmaster refused, in a tone which indicated he would brook no argument on the subject. "They're watching and, happen you *try* to do it—or *anything* else—they'll know straight away what you're up to and, at the very least, it could get Miz Betty killed afore Cap'n Fog can find her."

"Sam's *right*, Cy!" Maggie seconded, her voice angry. "We'll have to do what they want for now. But, by god, am I going to give them a *show* afore I let it look liked she's licked me."

"Just don't you get so all fired riled up you forget she's got to win!" Williams warned. "And keep one thing in mind. I know you took a 'mis-like' to each other as soon's you met, but that don't mean she's in on what's happening."

"She might not be, Maggie!" Bollinger supported, glancing to where the referee was carrying out the pre-contest examination of Big Ann Derby, watched by the two female members of her husband's wrestling troupe who were to serve as seconds. "Why'd you reckon the Bull's done it, Sam?"

"Could be finding out Big Ann couldn't do that trick Maggie pulled with the 'Monkey Ward dream book' got him worried she couldn't win," the postmaster guessed. "Or he might somehow've found out about them lessons in wrestling's Miz Betty 'n' Cap'n Fog've been giving you, Maggie. I'd say's the last's the more likely. Otherwise, they'd've grabbed off one or another of your kids and not her."

"Hey, Maggie," the referee said, returning from the other side of the ring. "Big Ann wants to know when you'll be ready to start?"

Although the speaker always acted in such a capacity for the wrestling and boxing bouts held in the Bull's Head Saloon, neither of the Bollingers nor Williams suspected him of complicity in the conspiracy. He lived locally, but was sufficiently wealthy that he was in no way dependent upon Keleney for his livelihood. Being aware of the way in which his victims might start thinking after having suffered losses from a betting coup, the town boss was too wily to have a proven confederate officiating at the event. Knowing this, despite the referee having delivered the message, the trio were satisfied that he could be counted upon to behave as fairly and impartially as was always the case in the past.

"I'm ready if she is, Fred," Maggie declared, extending her hands so the check of their fingernails could be made.

"Whatever you do," Williams counselled, after the referee had completed his examination and was returning to the centre of the ring, signalling for silence. "Keep it going's long's you can so's you'll give Cap'n Fog the chance to find out what's doing and come back."

"You can count on me to do *that!*" Maggie promised, eyeing her opponent coldly. "I don't like her and, even if she don't know what's doing, I wouldn't want to let it end afore she *knows* who's the better woman."

Announcing the combatants in turn, the referee called for them to join him. Having given them a quick explanation of the rules and warnings with regards to the use of illegal tactics, he told them to shake hands and return to their corners. Although Maggie held out her right hand, Ann slapped it aside with a contemptuous gesture and swung on her heel to walk away. Controlling her inclination to launch an immediate attack, the local woman did as she was ordered. Despite having watched for some indication, she could not decide whether her opponent was aware of the conspiracy.

Reaching their respective corners, the combatants limbered up briefly on the ropes. At the referee's command, they wasted no time in converging in the centre of the ring. It was obvious to the spectators that each was eager to come to grips with the other. As they drew close enough, their hands met and fingers intertwined. Pushing forward with her torso and legs, Maggie felt Ann responding in an identical fashion and knew she was engaged in a trial of strength. So evenly were they matched in that quality, their arms spread outwards as the feet and legs of each sought to shove the other backwards. Their bodies came together bosom to bosom and, being equally well endowed, they found themselves looking into one another's face.

"I told them I didn't need any help to lick you!" Ann asserted through gritted teeth, after a few seconds of exertion had produced no result on either side.

The comment achieved its purpose!

Surprised and angered by the admittance, Maggie could not avoid relaxing her efforts momentarily!

It was enough!

Taking advantage of the opportunity she had created, Ann thrust forward and drove her bent right leg upwards between her opponent's spread apart thighs!

"K—keep away from me!" Betty Hardin requested, cowering against the wall of the line cabin with well simulated abject terror.

Instead of complying, Joseph "Lil Joey" Cockburn extended his hands. His fingers and thumbs were crooked, ready to sink into and grind upon the firm mounds of the girl's breasts. Grinning viciously as he took in the sight of the apparent fear which she was displaying, he was savouring in anticipation the kind of enjoyment he was intending to have at her expense before killing her.

Being possessed of a sound judgement where human nature was concerned, Betty was forming accurate and disturbing deductions as she watched the play of lascivious emotions on the face of the jockey. Although she was far from being as terror stricken as was suggested by her demeanour, she did not doubt that she was in an extremely perilous situation.

Going by what Cockburn had said on his arrival, he was not acting upon the orders or even with the knowledge and consent of Daniel "Bull" Keleney. Yet, in spite of that, he had come to the cabin to avenge himself for the indignity he had suffered at the hands of her "husband." All of which suggested he was convinced he could rely upon his employer to shield him from the consequences of his actions. Therefore, despite her success in dealing with the two men who had abducted her, the girl decided that she would be wasting her time if she tried to employ similar tactics again.

Under the circumstances, Betty felt sure that learning the true identity of herself and her cousin was not going to persuade the jockey to desist. In fact, even in the *extremely* unlikely event that his original intentions had been merely to rape and leave her alive, such a disclosure might cause him to change his mind. Regardless of whether the plan to kill Dusty, about which he had hinted, was a success or a failure, Cockburn did not dare allow her to survive and be able to name him as her assailant. Nor would he consider his situation to be made worse by killing the granddaughter of Ole Devil Hardin rather than "Mrs. Elizabeth Silverstone" who, as far as was known, had no important family connections. As he had pointed out, her original abductors would be the obvious suspects for whatever he did to her. What was more, when presented with such a *fait accompli*—particularly if her true identity was told to him—a desire for self preservation would compel Keleney to order Town Marshal Hawley Grenville to ensure that the participation of the jockey in the crime was not established.

Having drawn her conclusions, the girl considered there was only one course left open to her. Nor was she deterred by the far from pleasant realization that, once she embarked upon it, there could be no turning back. Accepting this to be the case, she did all she could to improve her chances of survival.

Satisfied that she had succeeded in conveying an impression calculated to lure Cockburn into a state of over confidence, Betty went into action with swift and well thought out thoroughness. Shooting forward her right hand, she caught and bent back his thumb so his palm was turned upwards. Surprise, as much as pain shocked him into immobility as the abrupt change in her demeanour took him unawares. Hoping to prevent him from recovering his wits, she clenched her other fist in one of the ways she had been taught by Tommy Okasi and aimed for a target she had learned from the same source. Protruding ahead of the other three, it was the knuckle of the forefinger which made the primary contact. Not, unfortunately, upon the point at which it was directed.

Either chance or instinct had caused Cockburn to turn his head when his thumb was grasped. Although the blow he received just below the cheekbone was hard and hurt, he might have considered himself lucky. If he had been struck as the girl intended, the *hitsosashiyubi-ipponken*—"forefinger fist"—attack upon the *philtrum* collection of nerve centres just under the nose would have been at least incapacitating, or even fatal. As it was, he began to step back hurriedly if involuntarily and, his thumb being released, went sprawling on to his rump.

Despite having failed in her primary purpose, Betty intended to make the most of the opportunity she was being offered. Instead of continuing the attack, she thrust herself from against the wall as the jockey was going down. It was her intention to leave the cabin before he recovered and flee upon the horse which had brought him there. She did not succeed. Hurt though he was, Cockburn still retained sufficient possession of his faculties to respond. Grabbing as she was passing, while he failed to grasp her ankle, he caught the hem of her skirt. The material slipped from his clutching hands, but not before her equilibrium was destroyed.

With her balance lost, Betty was unable to prevent herself from going down. However, being a competent horsewoman, she had learned how to fall with the least chance of sustaining an injury. Alighting on the floor, she continued to roll across it until able to regain control of her movements. Coming to a halt on her back, she saw there was no time to spare in self congratulation. Already Cockburn was starting to rise and his face was so suffused by rage she knew she must take even more strenuous measures to protect herself. Coming to a sitting position, she made to attempt to stand. Her left hand snatched up the hem of the skirt and the right dipped to pluck the Remington Double Derringer from the holster in the top of the left boot's leg.

"Keep back!" the girl commanded, grasping the "bird's head" butt of the little weapon in both hands and drawing back the hammer as she took sight at the advancing man.

"Yeah?" the jockey snarled, reaching for his Colt and keeping moving.

Knowing she had no other choice, Betty squeezed the trigger. There was a spurt of flame from the upper of the Remington's superposed barrels. The .41 rimfire cartridge lacked any long range potential, but was adequate at the distance involved. Struck in the forehead by the bullet, Cockburn toppled backwards. Although the girl pulled back the hammer once more, she knew the threat to her life was over and she could go help her cousin.

CHAPTER SIXTEEN

Are You All Right, "Mr. Ed?"

The attack with which Big Ann Derby followed up her mocking comment was partially successful, but it failed to achieve its full potential. If she had been slightly further away from Maggie Bollinger, the solid bone of her knee would have been able to dictate the conduct of at least the remainder of the first fall. As it was, however, only the firm muscular flesh of her thigh slammed into the crotch of the local woman. Despite the result being somewhat less severe than would otherwise have been the case, Maggie was driven to retreat and she could not prevent her left arm being twisted behind her back in a painful hammerlock. Thrust against the tightly stretched ropes, she felt their tension being added to the impulsion with which she was jerked from them and flipped through the air to alight on her back in the centre of the ring. She had only one thing for which to feel thankful. Whilst in flight, she was able to swing her left arm clear. Instead of it being crushed beneath her when she landed, she used it to help reduce the force of her arrival on the canvas.

As they had been instructed, the employers of the Bull's Head Saloon and the others of Daniel "Bull" Keleney's adherents had set up such a clamour it led those about them to join in with much louder encouragement for the combatants than would usually have been the case so early in a bout. Listening to the growing volume of noise, Samuel Williams became even more concerned for the safety of Dusty Fog. He felt certain that the commotion was intended to prevent anybody in the bar-room hearing shooting from outside the building. Having reached this conclusion, and watching what was taking place in the ring, he also wondered whether it would meet with the approval of the town boss.

Darting swiftly after her opponent, Ann dug both hands into the black hair. Hauled upright, Maggie was bent backwards in a head chancery. Before she could even try to counter the move, she was held by the left arm around her neck and the right was swung to strike her bosom, knocking her down. Almost as soon as her rump hit the canvas, she was once again pulled to her feet and felled in a similar fashion. However, on raising her for the third time, the red head changed tactics. Obtaining a hammerlock on Maggie's right arm, Ann passed her left over to apply a choking pressure to the other's wind pipe from behind. The hold was legal under the rules and, if retained, would quickly have rendered its recipient unconscious.

Realizing the danger posed by the hold and knowing such an early conclusion to the bout was far from desirable for a number of reasons, Keleney threw a warning glare at Willis Derby. However, before the promoter could catch his wife's eye and signal, the need to do so was removed.

Although shaken and somewhat bewildered by the brief onslaught, Maggie was equally alert to the peril. Determined to avoid being defeated, particularly with such apparent ease, she hooked her right foot behind Ann's right ankle and pulled forward at it, while shoving with the rest of her body in the opposite direction. Caught unprepared, the red head was unable to keep her balance. Feeling herself toppling backwards, Ann had no time to try to avoid what she knew was coming. Nor was she able to release her holds in an attempt to break the fall before she landed with the local woman on top of her. This, however, caused Maggie no inconvenience. Crushing Ann against the well padded canvas floor of the ring, against which the back of her head had landed hard enough to momentarily stun her, the local woman felt a weakening of the two grips. Snatching free her trapped wrist, she twisted over until they were face to face despite the other arm remaining about her neck. To complete the escape, she forced forward with her legs until she was able to arch her torso upward and could thrust her right knee into Ann's lower belly. Giving vent to a pain filled gasping squeal, the red head snatched her arm away involuntarily. Making the most of her liberty, Maggie plunged forward and twisted until her chest lay across and obscured Ann's head and shoulders.

As the referee was kneeling beside the combatants to ensure both of the red head's shoulders were pinned to the canvas before starting to count, Williams surmised that a fall at that time might not be to their advantage. There would be a cessation of the noise while the obligatory couple of minutes rest was granted prior to the commencement of the second fall. If there was shooting outside, it would be heard and, to keep up appearances, Keleney was likely to send some of his men to "investigate." This could lead to the discovery that "Edward Silverstone" had escaped the trap laid for him, giving him further difficulties and, possibly, causing the death of Betty Hardin. Seeing Maggie looking his way, he made a motion with his hands which he hoped she would interpret correctly.

Drawing the required conclusions and guessing why the signal had been made, Maggie relaxed the pressure she was exerting slightly. The moment she did, she had cause to regret the action. Seizing the opportunity, Ann opened her mouth to bite at the breast which had been rammed into her face and restricting her breathing. A pain-filled yelp burst from the local woman, the cloth offering little protection against such an attack. Jerking herself into a kneeling position, she lashed a back-handed slap to the side of the redhead's face. Before either of them could do any more, guessing what had happened, the referee shoved Maggie away from Ann and, coming to his feet, ordered them to rise.

Standing up, the combatants rubbed at the respectively smarting areas of their bodies. Then glaring in anger, they closed to go into the traditional "bulling" hold with the left hand gripping the back of the opponent's neck and the right on the shoulder.

"All right, you bitch!" Maggie gritted, as she and Ann swung around straining to take the advantage. "You've asked

for it. By the time I'm through with you, everybody's going to
know I had to let you win."

"Like hell I need you to *let* me!" the red head replied, just
as savagely. "When they carry you out of here, you're going
to wish you'd never come in the first place!"

"Help, somebody's robbing the schoolhouse!"

Listening to the shouted words, followed by the slamming
of the front door which they heard being opened a few seconds earlier, Neal Kinnock and Brock Fennerway exchanged
glances.

Dressed in cowhand style clothing, although nobody who
knew the West would take them for other than what they were,
the pair were neither the best nor the most intelligent of the
fraternity who lived by hiring out their skills with a gun. In
fact, under normal conditions, Daniel "Bull" Keleney would
not have considered them worthy of employing. However,
when they had arrived at his ranch in response to the word he
had put out that he needed assistance in another matter—
which had fallen through without the need arising—he had
seen a way he believed they might be of use. He had concluded they were not as smart and competent as the two men
taken on to abduct the wife of "Edward Silverstone," but felt
they would serve his purpose in another capacity. Sent to the
schoolhouse, they carried out the first part of the instructions
they received. Unfortunately, the sound of property being
destroyed in the living quarters had not caused their intended
victim to behave in the required fashion. Instead, it appeared
he had taken flight with the intention of raising the alarm.

"Come on, Brock!" Kinnock snarled, going through the
open door into the classroom with the weapon he had been
given in his hands.

"Don't forget you've got to down him with Moe's rifle!"
Fennerway warned, following so quickly that he caught up
with and advanced along the aisle between the desks at his
companion's side.

Although there was sufficient light for the pair to be able to
see the closed main door, most of the room lay in shadowy
gloom. The lack of visibility did not worry either of them.
With the suggestion that the "schoolteacher" for whom they
were waiting had run away, they did not consider there was

any need for vigilance and their only thought was to get within shooting distance before his behaviour brought people to investigate. It did not occur to them to wonder why "Silverstone" was no longer yelling in an attempt to summon aid.

Which proved to be a serious mistake!

A whistle had attracted the attention of the Bollinger twins and their brother before they could go into the schoolhouse. Dusty Fog approaching, they had obeyed the sign he made indicating he wished them to join him. On their arrival, he had appraised them of the situation and had given instructions. While speaking, he had removed his jacket and necktie. Thankful that he had decided to wear it, as its colour would be less noticeable than if he had selected one of white, he had opened the attached collar of his grey flannel shirt. In contrast to the noise he had made as he entered the building, he had shown great stealth while making his way to crouch between two of the desks on the right side of the aisle. Having done so without being detected by the men in the living quarters, he had yelled the words which were a signal for Cyrus Junior to slam the front door and add to the impression he wished to create.

Waiting until the unsuspecting pair had just gone by, the small Texan lunged from his place of concealment. Although the left leg was nearer, reaching across, he caught hold of Fennerway's right ankle and jerked it towards him. The tug gave its recipient an off balance spin and, as he was going down, he crashed as was intended into his companion. Knocked staggering by the unexpected impact which came as he had one foot raised, Kinnock inadvertently tugged at the trigger of the Winchester Model of 1873 rifle he was carrying. It fired and the recoil served to break his already relaxing hold. With the weapon slipping from his grasp, he was unable to prevent himself from falling across the last desk on the left side of the aisle. Nor, losing his hat as he went, was the other would-be killer any better able to avoid sprawling on hands and knees in front of the door.

"I'm all right!" Dusty snapped, seeing the front door start to open. "Stay put out there!"

While speaking, the small Texan was going towards the nearer of his intended killers. Much to his relief, whichever of the Bollinger children had meant to enter obeyed his order and

none of them forgot that he had said for them to remain silent
no matter what they heard from inside the building.

Bewildered by the unanticipated turn of events, Kinnock
felt himself grabbed by the scruff of the neck and waist belt.
Before he could decide upon some means of retaliation, much
less attempt to put it into effect, he was hauled from the desk
by what was clearly an exceptionally strong person. Exerting
all the power his miniature Herculean frame could produce,
Dusty swung around and flung the man across the room.
Unable to stop himself, Kinnock tripped over his companion
and crashed into the wall with sufficient force to be rendered
unconscious.

Nor did Fennerway fare any better. Never among the
quickest of thinkers in his chosen field of endeavour, his far
from active brain had not caught up with the train of events
which he was assaulted by—although he did not know it—
his companion. The impact sent him flat on his face and his
position was far from improved by having Kinnock rebound
from the wall to fall on top of him. For all that, alarmed by
what had taken place, and even though he could not imagine
how it had come about, he began to try to struggle free.

Striding forward with the intention of ensuring that both of
his would-be assailants were rendered *hors de combat*, Dusty
picked up the rifle dropped by Kinnock in passing. He had
questions he wanted to ask and considered the weapon might
provide an aid to producing the answers. However, before he
reached the two men, he remembered what had been said
about the use to which the Winchester must be put and the
name of its owner. Adding this information to the recollection
of the comments made by Samuel Williams about the way in
which the previous schoolteacher had been murdered, and to
his own thoughts on the absence of a prominent Keleney
adherent from the Bull's Head Saloon, he began to consider a
disturbing possibility.

Even as the small Texan was reaching the conclusions, he
heard footsteps crossing the living quarters from the second
door. Swinging around, he decided his summations were correct. Carrying a double barrelled ten gauge shotgun, Town
Marshal Hawley Grenville strode across the threshold of the
classroom. However, despite the addition to his armament, his
behaviour was not that of a competent peace officer—which
Dusty knew him to be, for all his acceptance of orders from

Keleney—coming to investigate a disturbance. Instead of making a quiet approach and looking cautiously around the edge of the door, he had come straight onto the scene of a shooting. Which implied he considered it was safe for him to do so.

There could be only one reason for such confidence!

Grenville knew what was supposed to have happened!

And had been told what to do on finding the ambush was successful!

"They didn't get y—!" the peace officer began, coming to a halt and staring along the aisle.

The unfinished comment was not inspired by relief!

In spite of the shock he had received from the discovery that the intended victim had not only survived but was armed, Grenville reacted swiftly. Carried in a position of readiness, he swung the butt of the shotgun to his shoulder with the deft speed of long practise while making the potentially incriminating declaration.

Having guessed the reason for the peace officer's arrival, Dusty had also surmised the response which the changed situation would elicit. Knowing his life was in danger, he acted with his usual speed and forethought. While he held the Winchester, and its weight suggested there were bullets in the tubular magazine beneath the barrel, it had been fired and there was only an empty case in the chamber. Replacing this with a live round could be achieved swiftly enough, but the rifle had been dropped and its mechanism might have been damaged. Having no desire to conduct an experiment in such an exposed position, he dived to the floor behind the left side desk.

The evasive action was not a moment too soon!

Flame erupted from the right and left hand barrels of the shotgun in rapid succession. However, so well timed had been the movement of the small Texan, the peace officer was unable to make the necessary adjustment to the point of aim. For all that, as he landed on the floor, Dusty heard some of the eighteen .32 calibre buckshot balls strike the desk behind which he had disappeared. The rest made a pattern of pock marks on the wall, but he was confident it was thick enough to prevent them passing through and endangering the Bollinger children.

Operating the lever of the Winchester, the small Texan was

relieved to feel it moving smoothly and with nothing to suggest the mechanism had been affected. The breech cover slid back and allowed the empty case to be ejected and he saw a charged bullet being fed into the chamber. Satisfied, he thrust himself into a kneeling position and swung the rifle's barrel over the top of the desk while bringing the butt to his shoulder. One glance told him he was going to need it.

Watching "Silverstone" going down as he was firing, Grenville was satisfied that he had made a hit. Although the situation was not as he and Keleney had envisaged, he did not consider the plan was now unworkable. It had been his intention to shoot the two men so their bodies and the Winchester could be exhibited as "proof " that the murderers of Orville Webster and the "new schoolteacher" had paid the penalty for their crimes. This, he considered, could still be done with only a few modifications to the story of what had taken place.

Breaking open the shotgun, the peace officer resumed his advance along the aisle with the intention of carrying out the amendment to the scheme. The distinctive sound of a Winchester's action being operated from where "Silverstone" had disappeared warned him that all might not be as satisfactory as he had assumed. At the sight of the "new schoolteacher" rising apparently unscathed, he completed the reloading as swiftly as he could and tried to use the weapon to defend himself.

Aiming along the barrel of the rifle rather than making use of its sights, Dusty fired in the only way he dared under the circumstances. Not only was he handling an unfamiliar weapon, but there was insufficient light and time to permit the accuracy required for making a hit which would merely incapacitate the peace officer. Accepting the inevitable, but hoping for the best, he squeezed the trigger. The hope did not come to fruition. Flying by chance rather than deliberate intention, the bullet ripped into Grenville's left breast and tore through his heart to kill him instantly. Spun around by the impact of the lead, with the shotgun flying from his grasp, his lifeless body disappeared between two of the desks.

Despite considering he had nothing further to fear from the peace officer, Dusty was too experienced in such matters to leave this to chance. Coming to his feet, however, he saw there was something else demanding his attention before he could go and check upon Grenville's condition. Spurred by alarm over what he had seen and heard, Fennerway had contrived to wriggle from beneath Kinnock and was sitting up. Although he did not pose any threat as yet, the small Texan had no intention of permitting him to develop into one. Stepping forward, he swung the Winchester one handed in a horizontal arc. Catching Fennerway on the side of the head, the octagonal barrel knocked him senseless and he flopped limply on to his back.

"Are you all right, 'Mr. Ed?'" Cyrus Junior called, opening the front door a trifle.

"Sure," Dusty replied, without taking his attention from where Grenville had fallen. "Go fetch me some rope, then head on home and stay there."

Propelled by the springiness of the ropes, half blinded by copious perspiration and swaying in exhaustion, Maggie Bollinger hurtled across the ring with little control over her movements. A sensation of consternation arose as she realized that, looking in no better condition, Big Ann Derby was coming straight at her in a similarly hasty and unguided fashion.

It would have been a very hard to please spectator who felt disappointed or dissatisfied by the bout of wrestling which had taken place over the past thirty minutes. Going at it without a pause, except when one or the other was down and being counted, they had given of their best, and respectively taken all that was being inflicted in return. What was more, it had soon become obvious that neither considered she was engaged in a mere sporting contest to be ended by a pinfall. Instead, they had directed all their attention and efforts towards trying to force a submission in the most painful manner.

After their exchange of threats while "bulling," Maggie had contrived to send Ann crashing to the mat with a combined headlock and cross buttock. Her attempt to capitalize on the momentary advantage had been brought to an end with her head caught in a scissors from which she escaped, after taking some punishment, by struggling vigorously. As soon as they had regained their feet, they went at it hammer and tongs. Throws, holds and their counters, were freely mingled with some kneeing, butting, punching and hair pulling, all exchanged with savage abandon.

Early in the struggle, the referee had intervened when Ann's behaviour had led to them both contravening the rules by grasping and working upon the other's breasts like a baker kneading bread for the oven. When he was compelled to haul them apart by the hair, they had turned upon him and left him in no doubt that there was a limit to how much control over their conduct they would permit him to exert. Thereafter, knowing the crowd would not be willing to allow such an exciting contest to be ended by the disqualification of either woman—even if they would agree to such a ruling themselves—he had kept clear of them and contented himself with doing nothing more than counting when one or the other was sent down in a way which could have resulted in a knockout.

Possessed of a mutual disinclination towards suffering even a one fall defeat, Maggie and Ann had taken punishment which in a normal bout would have led the recipient to seek the respite offered by submission. Freed from official restraint by the referee, when in difficulty, they were granted a liberty to employ means of escape which would otherwise have caused disqualification. Of the two, however, the red head's methods were most open to criticism. Her use of a clenched fist to the bosom or crotch as an aid to escape from a potential submission hold were more clearly violations of the rules than the open handed *karate* thrusts, jabs or chops which the local woman had been taught by Dusty Fog and Betty Hardin. On the other hand, Ann had one advantage which had served to extract her from trouble when other means failed. Twice she had found herself trapped in such a way that she could find no physical counter. Each time, a warning of what would happen to the "schoolma'am" if she should lose had compelled her opponent to set her free.

As the bout had progressed, the red head had found herself growing increasingly grateful for the control which the abduction allowed her to exert. Her earlier confidence had become shaken by the discovery that she had a far smaller margin of superior wrestling skill than she had assumed would be the case. What was more, the local woman was proving to be stronger and had a slight advantage in size and weight which did much to counter her extra ability. To add to Ann's discomfiture and consternation, she found the other possessed ways of inducing pain with the fingers and edge of the hand which were beyond her ken. All in all, she was now far from being as disdainful of the precautions taken to ensure her victory than she had been when entering the ring.

On her part, Maggie was under the restriction of being unable to go all out for victory. Even without the various reminders from Ann, she had been constantly aware that the life of Betty Hardin was in her hands. This was the main reason for her determination to prevent the bouts from going beyond a single fall. Not only had the red head threatened to refuse to come out for a second if compelled to concede the first, but she doubted whether she could continue to restrain her temper should she have to yield in a way which would require the bout to go on. Having this in mind, in addition to a desire to inflict as much punishment upon Ann as possible before having to let herself be defeated, she had driven herself to keep going no matter how much suffering was being inflicted upon her.

Chance rather than any deliberately planned movement on either's part had set both women careering wildly back and forth across the ring. In their exhausted state, neither was able to halt her progress or to do more than turn their backs to the ropes an instant before arriving and being propelled away again. Letting out breathless wails of alarm as an appreciation of their mutual danger struck them, they came together with a resounding thud. For a moment, they stood pressed face to face, bosom to bosom, belly to belly and thigh to thigh. Then, slowly and seemingly reluctantly, their touching foreheads separated and, peeling apart like a split banana skin, they toppled on to their backs.

Not until the count was half over could Maggie make her aching body respond to the dictates of her mind. Rolling on to her stomach, oblivious of the excited clamour from the spectators, she forced her head and torso upwards. A glance told her that Ann was also struggling to rise. For a moment, she tried to compel obedience from her protesting frame. Then she realized this could be the opportunity she needed. Although Dusty Fog had not returned, she knew both she and the red head were almost completely spent. It was unlikely that either of them could keep going for much longer and, in her present state, she might easily knock the other unconscious without meaning to. However, if Ann could beat the count, and she stayed down, the fight would end as required by Keleney.

CHAPTER SEVENTEEN

Keleney Can Read

Assailed by a sense of mortification which threatened to bring tears to her eyes, Maggie Bollinger started to let herself sink towards the canvas. Behind her and unseen, panting for breath and clearly making a terrific effort, Big Ann Derby continued to struggle towards standing up. Seeing what was happening, those of the spectators who were betting on the local woman —and, due to the information supplied by the two men at the stage depot, they were in the majority among the crowd— groaned in disappointment as she began to subside.

At the ring-side table, Willis Derby directed a glance filled with a relief at Daniel "Bull" Keleney. Neither had been enamoured of the way in which the bout was being conducted. There had been more than one occasion when it seemed Maggie had forgotten her instructions and meant to administer a *coup de grace*. Now it appeared she either could not get up or had decided to avoid endangering the life of Betty Hardin and was allowing herself to be counted out.

Standing on the apron outside the corner of the local woman, Cyrus Bollinger and Sam Williams exchanged looks redolent of their disappointment. Having drawn similar conclusions to those of Keleney, each had much the same thought as their eyes met. Once again, it seemed the town boss would pull off a betting coup. Nor, as they had seen and heard nothing from the small Texan, could either think of any way in which they might prevent this from happening.

Just before her face reached the floor, Maggie's attention was drawn to a man who had contrived to pass through the crowd and was stepping towards the ring. Even in her distressed and enfeebled condition, she swiftly became aware of what was implied by the sight. Not only had Captain Fog returned, but as soon as he saw he had been noticed by her, his lips moved. Although she could not hear what was said, a sense of elation tore through her as she realized the words were, "Betty's safe!"

The information gave Maggie all the inducement she needed. A surge of satisfaction and relief passed through her, overwhelming the pain and exhaustion which was assailing her. Such was the vigour she expended in thrusting herself from the canvas, she was on her feet as quickly as the red head.

Having derived comfort and solace from seeing the local woman apparently collapsing in defeat, Ann gave vent to a croaking gasp of consternation at the change. She had been so close to giving up herself, only the belief that her opponent was finished had supplied the goad to help her rise. The discovery that she was in error drove through her like an icy blast. Nor did the expression on her opponent's haggard, sweat-soddened face do anything to improve her state of mind. Rather the effect was most frightening and destroyed all her will to continue.

Such was the boost to Maggie's morale by the return of Dusty Fog, she no longer felt on the verge of collapse. Instead, as Ann stumbled backwards on legs which looked as unsteady as heat buckled candles and with her arms held out in a gesture closer to pleading that readiness for defence, she advanced with vigorously determined strides. For all that, she was acting on instinct and not conscious thought as she caught the red head's wrist in both hands. Jerking at the trapped limb, she began to turn and swing Ann around like the weight at the bottom of a pendulum. Having rotated four times with an ever increasing momentum, she released her grip. Despite the sudden cessation of the strain to which she had been subjected causing her to stagger, she contrived to halt without falling.

Standing on spread apart feet, hands on hips and breast heaving as she fought to replenish her lungs with air, she exerted all her will power to stave off the flood of exhaustion which was returning.

Ann was far less fortunate. On being liberated, the impetus acquired during the circular motion to which she had been subjected sent her hurtling off at a tangent. Because of the speed at which she was moving, she was helpless to avoid or even try to counter what she sensed was coming. On colliding with the ropes, the top strand bent under her weight without restraining her onwards progression. Instead, it acted as a pivot around which she rolled as her feet left the mat. Turning a half somersault, with her head striking the edge of the apron in passing, she tumbled to the floor. Eager hands lifted and pushed her back into the ring, but not even the most optimistic onlooker believed she would be able to beat the count.

"Why the hell did she do th—?" Bollinger breathed, staring in consternation from the sprawled out and unmoving red head to his wife and back.

"Cap'n Fog must've got back!" Williams guessed, being unable to see the small Texan from where he was standing. Nodding to the box at their feet, he went on, "Which being, we'd best take that with us and go get set to help him!"

"Well now, Mr. Keleney. I'd say things've gone more than a mile wrong for *you* this time, wouldn't you?"

Despite the tumultuous reception being given to the announcement from the referee that Maggie Bollinger had won the wrestling bout by a knockout, the town boss heard the comment that was directed at him. However, such was his anger over the result, he failed to appreciate the full implication of the words at first. When the relization of what was said and by whom struck him, he wondered if his ears were playing a trick upon him, and he turned to face the speaker. Not only did he discover he had heard correctly, but there was a further shock awaiting him. In addition to having escaped unscathed from the ambush at the schoolhouse, "Edward Silverstone" now wore a gunbelt of excellent design and manufacture, with a brace of white handled Colt Civilian Model Peacemakers in its cross-draw holsters.

As on the night when Orville Webster was murdered,

nobody had come to investigate the shooting at the school-house. After having secured the two unconscious hired killers with the rope provided by the Bollinger children, Dusty Fog had ascertained that Town Marshal Hawley Grenville was dead. Satisfied on that point, he had gone into the living quarters. There had been some damage done, but he and his cousin had brought nothing that was valuable or irreplaceable with them and the hiding place beneath the bed had not been discovered. Retrieving and donning the weapons concealed therein, he had returned to the classroom.

On recovering and being told what would have happened to them if they had carried out their assignment, Neal Kinnock and Brock Fennerway had sworn vengeance against Keleney. With this in mind and having been informed of the small Texan's true identity, which they were led to believe was known to the town boss, they had declared they were willing to testify in court that they had been acting on his orders. Warning them of the consequences if they should slip their bonds and try to escape, Dusty had heard a horse approaching rapidly as he was collecting the Winchester rifle to take with him to the Bull's Head Saloon.

Arriving on the lathered and leg weary animal she had appropriated at the line cabin, Betty Hardin had told her cousin of what had happened to her. The information she had gleaned from her captors, particularly about Three Socks being at the ranch owned by Keleney, had been further evidence which could be used against him should he be brought to trial. They had also concluded that, if subjected to the right kind of pressure, Ezekiel Barnesley could be induced to help incriminate his employer. However, wanting to ensure they had as strong a case as possible, Dusty suggested another means of doing so. This had entailed breaking into the post office and obtaining an item essential to his scheme.

Suspecting that the town boss would be disinclined to yield peaceably to a citizen's arrest, the small Texan had considered it inadvisable for his cousin to enter the saloon with him. Instead, armed with the Winchester, she had remained just outside the open main entrance so as to keep watch on the men occupying the balcony. Knowing he could rely upon her to keep him covered from that direction, he had gone into the bar-room and discovered that he had arrived at a critical moment of the wrestling bout. Having delivered the news which encouraged Maggie Bollinger to rise and defeat Big Ann Derby, he had passed around the ring to bring about the showdown with the town boss.

"Yeah, 'Silverstone,'" Keleney growled, alarmed by this latest turn of events. "It looks like things have at that."

"It's mighty lucky for most of these fellers that those two jaspers brought word of what happened in Brownsville," Dusty went on, halting with his hands dangling loosely by his sides. In spite of this, he conveyed the impression of being as tense and ready for motion as a compressed coil spring. "Only they spread the word that the wrong gal won the wrestling match down there."

While speaking, the small Texan saw from the corner of his eye that Williams and Bollinger were crossing the ring. They were carrying the first aid box between them, but were not making for where Maggie was supporting herself on the ropes. Instead, the lid of the container was raised and each had his right hand inside and he knew they were coming to support him.

"How'd you mean?" Keleney asked, flickering glances to where Brick Shatterhouse and Moe Broody—who were aware of what was supposed to happen to the "new schoolteacher"— had moved to stand on either side of him.

"I thought it was just a mite too coincidental for them to drop like they did," Dusty explained and held forward the buff coloured telegraph message form which he had collected from the post office. "So I sent word to my uncle—he's sheriff of Cameron County—asking who had won. He telegraphed back that Big Ann licked the Countess so easily there was like to be a riot. This's his message."

Watching what was happening, those members of the crowd closest to the group sensed impending danger. It was common knowledge around Grattan that there was no love lost between Keleney and the "new schoolteacher." Despite the apparently relaxed way in which the latter was standing, the fact that he was wearing guns for the first time since his arrival and the attitudes of the men he was confronting were clear indication of trouble in the air. Aware of the possible threat to themselves as innocent bystanders, the nearest of the onlookers fell silent and began to edge away from the vicinity of the possible confrontation. Their behaviour affected those around them, until it spread all through the room with a speed which would have amazed anybody unfamiliar with dwellers west of the Mississippi River and their response to such situations. In a remarkably short while, there was hardly a sound from the hitherto rowdy crowd and everybody was waiting to find out what was happening. Even Willis Derby and Doctor Cornelius Manneheim considered it advisable to withdraw and edged away from the ringside table.

Conscious that he was a major part of the centre of attraction, Keleney accepted the folded sheet of paper from the small Texan. Instead of commenting upon his illiteracy, as was his habit when offered something which might require reading, he opened and looked at it.

"There's nothing about the fight here!" the town boss burst out before he could stop himself.

"I *know* there isn't," Dusty replied, having hoped to provoke some such reaction and concluding that the delay incurred by acquiring the necessary document had been justified. "It said, 'Keleney can read and write!'"[1]

"Get him!" the town boss bellowed, letting the incriminating telegraph form slip from his fingers and reaching for the revolver in his shoulder holster.

More experienced than their employer in such matters, Shatterhouse and Broody had been studying the small Texan carefully. Neither cared for the conclusions he had drawn. Without the need for consultation, each had decided that "Edward Silverstone" was a force to be reckoned with. For one thing, his gunbelt bore the unmistakable quality produced by the man said to be the finest leather worker in Texas and it was common knowledge that old Joe Gaylin of El Paso only offered his superlative rigs to very carefully selected tophands in matters *pistolero*. Going by the way it fitted, the one worn by "Silverstone" had been made for him. Which implied he was something far more than an unimportant schoolteacher. It also meant he would be fully capable of holding up his end in

---

1 *Anxious to save himself from prosecution, Ezekiel Barnesley declared that Daniel "Bull" Keleney was not illiterate. An examination of his business documents established it was he who wrote the messages received by Dusty Fog and Samuel Williams. J.T.E.*

any company should gunplay occur.

With that in mind, the two hard cases commenced their draws as soon as Keleney gave the order.

At the same moment, other members of the town boss's coterie prepared to join the fray if they should be needed.

The men on the balcony dropped their hands to the butts of guns. Being too far away to have duplicated the conclusions Shatterhouse and Broody had formed, they foresaw no trouble from "Silverstone" and were making ready to deal with any hostility on the part of the crowd.

Observing the behaviour of the onlookers, Bernie—his head swathed in a bandage—and the other bartenders had climbed on to the counter so as to be able to look over the heads of the crowd. As was his habit when there was a possibility of danger, Bernie was grasping a sawed off shotgun ready for use.

Terry Parry was never invited to sit at the ring-side table, but he had followed his usual practice of getting as close to it as possible and had remained in the forefront of the crowd. Although he started to draw his gun, it was not intended to be employed against the "new schoolteacher." Sharing the belief of the men on the balcony that "Silverstone" would be killed without the need of his intervention, he had decided to make the most of his opportunity by paving the way for his promotion to postmaster. Eager to attain his ambition, he was directing his attention towards Williams in the ring and waiting for an excuse to start shooting.

Flashing across on the first movement of Keleney's mouth, as he had deduced what order would be given, Dusty's hands scooped the Colts from their carefully designed holsters. Such was his completely ambidextrous prowess that, in just over half a second from the commencement of the draw, the four and three-quarter inch barrels had swung outwards at waist level and the weapons roared in unison. The guns of neither Shatterhouse nor Broody had cleared leather and were given no chance to do so. At almost the same instant as the former took a bullet in the throat from the small Texan's left hand revolver, the latter was hit between the eyes.

Shocked by the display of devastating speed, Keleney hesitated!

It was a fatal error!

Turning as if their muzzles were attracted by a magnetic force, Dusty's matched brace of Colts—their hammers having been cocked on the recoil—roared again. Caught in the chest by both bullets, the town boss was thrown backwards between the collapsing bodies of Shatterhouse and Broody. He joined them in crashing lifeless on to the floor.

Taken completely unawares by the way in which the affair had developed, none of the town boss's adherents were capable of responding with their usual alacrity. Not until they saw Keleney, Shatterhouse and Broody going down did any of them offer to rectify the situation.

Starting to bring out his revolver, one of the men on the balcony was prevented by a bullet in the head from the Winchester in the hands of Betty Hardin.[2] Having been positioned by Williams to cope with such a contingency, Walter "Trader" Staines produced the sawed off shotgun he had concealed beneath his jacket and felled a second hard-case with a blow to the head from its barrels. Having done so, he swung the weapon ready to quell any further opposition in his immediate vicinity.

Discarding the first aid box in which the weapons had been hidden, the elderly postmaster and Bollinger each put the Colt 1860 Army revolver he was grasping to action.

Showing he still possessed much of the skill acquired while serving with the Texas Light Cavalry, the blacksmith raised his revolver in both hands. Sighting swiftly and firing, he made Bernie his mark. The .44 calibre round soft lead ball was driven into the stomach of the bartender, twirling him from the counter. Although his shotgun bellowed as he went, its potentially lethal charge passed harmlessly over the heads of the crowd and nowhere near the target for which it had been intended.

2 *Alvin Dustine "Cap" Fog has explained why there was no reference to the participation of Betty Hardin in the source upon which our original record of the events herein was based. The omission came about as a result of the earlier generation of the Hardin, Fog and Blaze clan being disinclined to admit that, even though the circumstances were completely justifiable in each case, she had twice been compelled to take the life of another human being. J.T.E.*

Knowing something of Parry's ambitions, Williams had kept him under surveillance. Discovering his misgivings were correct, the postmaster experienced a well justified sense of satisfaction as he directed a bullet which—by accident rather than design—broke the right elbow of his treacherous assistant and removed the threat to his life.

"The name's Dusty Fog!" announced the small Texan, in the silence which descended after the thunder of shots had come to an end. "I've killed Bull Keleney and I'm ready to face *anybody* who wants to take it up for him!"

There was no reply!

Studying the deliverer of the challenge, who had ceased to appear small in stature and insignificant, nobody doubted he was the famous man he had claimed to be. Nor did anybody consider he would be unwilling, or unable, to back his play if his bet should be called.

Standing with the smoke still rising lazily from the barrels of the cocked Colts in his hands, Dusty threw a glance around. Various members of the population, including some who would have been at least tacit supporters of Keleney under different circumstances, were covering and ensuring there would be no further intervention by the surviving members of the saloon's staff. At the front doors, Betty Hardin was still cradling the Winchester at her shoulder and aided by Staines, was keeping the hard-cases on the balcony under control. In the ring, tucking the Army Colt into his waistband, Bollinger was crossing to where his wife stood over her unconscious opponent, using the ropes to keep her on her feet. Williams did not follow, but was conducting a survey similar to that of the small Texan.

"Looks like we've got our town back, Cap'n Fog," the elderly postmaster asserted, gazing over the ropes at the conclusion of his scrutiny, being satisfied there would be no further hostility.

"That's how it is, Sam," Dusty agreed. "You'll be needing a new schoolteacher, though. Cousin Betty and I have to be getting back to the OD Connected now it's over."

"We'll be right sorry to see you go, grown-ups and kids alike," Williams declared. "And finding somebody' them young cusses'll get on so well with won't be easy."

"Why won't it?" Dusty objected. "Hell, Sam, I'm not a schoolteacher."

"Maybe not," Williams answered, then glanced at the three lifeless bodies sprawled in front of the small Texan. "But there's nobody's can say right truthful's you aren't a master of 'triggernometry.'"

Appendix One

Following his enrollment in the Army of the Confederate States,[1] Dustine Edward Marsden "Dusty" Fog had won promotion to captain in the field by the time he reached his seventeenth birthday and was put in command of Company "C," Texas Light Cavalry.[2] Leading them throughout the Arkansas' campaign, he had earned the reputation of being an exceptionally capable military raider and a worthy, if junior, contemporary of the South's other leading exponents of what eventually became known as "commando" tactics,[3] Turner Ashby and John Singleton "the Grey Ghost" Mosby.[4] In addition to preventing a pair of pro-Union fanatics from starting an Indian uprising which would have decimated much of Texas,[5] he had

1 *Details of some of Dusty Fog's activities prior to his enrollment are given in:* Part Five, The Civil War series, "A Time For Improvisation, Mr. Blaze," J.T.'S HUNDREDTH.

2 *Told in:* YOU'RE IN COMMAND NOW, MR. FOG.

3 *The first "commandos" were bands of South African irregular troops fighting the British in the Boer War.*

4 *Told in:* THE BIG GUN, UNDER THE STARS AND BARS, THE FASTEST GUN IN TEXAS *and* KILL DUSTY FOG!

5 *Told in:* THE DEVIL GUN.

supported Belle "the Rebel Spy" Boyd on two of her most dangerous assignments.[6]

At the conclusion of the War Between The States, Dusty became segundo of the great OD Connected ranch in Rio Hondo County, Texas. Its owner and his paternal uncle, General Jackson Baines "Ole Devil" Hardin, C.S.A., had been crippled in a riding accident,[7] placing much responsibility upon his young shoulders. This had included handling an important mission upon which the future relations between the United States and Mexico depended.[8] While doing so, he had been helped by the two men who became his best friends and leading lights of the ranch's floating outfit,[9] Mark Counter and the Ysabel Kid.[10] Aided by them, he had helped gather horses to replenish the ranch's *remuda*,[11] then was sent to assist Colonel Charles Goodnight on the trail drive to Fort Sumner, New Mexico, which had done much to help the Lone Star State recover from the impoverished conditions left by the War.[12]

6 *Told in:* THE COLT AND THE SABRE *and* THE REBEL SPY. *Other details of Belle "The Rebel Spy" Boyd's career are given in:* THE BLOODY BORDER, BACK TO THE BLOODY BORDER, THE HOODED RIDERS, THE BAD BUNCH, SET A-FOOT, TO ARMS! TO ARMS! IN DIXIE!, THE SOUTH WILL RISE AGAIN, THE QUEST FOR BOWIE'S BLADE, Part Eight, Belle "The Rebel Spy" Boyd, Affair of Honour," J.T.'S HUNDREDTH *and* Part Five, The Butcher's Fiery End," J.T.'S LADIES.

7 *Told in the* "The Paint," THE FASTEST GUN IN TEXAS. *Further details of General Hardin's career are given in the* Ole Devil Hardin *and* The Civil War series *and his death is reported in:* DOC LEROY, M.D.

8 *Told in:* YSABEL KID.

9 "Floating Outfit": *a group of four to six cowhands employed by a large ranch to work the more distant sections of the property. Taking food in a chuck wagon, or "greasy sack" on the back of a mule, they would be away from the ranch house for long periods and so were the pick of the crew. Because of General Hardin's prominence in the affairs of Texas, the OD Connected's floating outfit were frequently sent to assist such of his friends who found themselves in difficulties or endangered.*

10 *Details of the careers of Mark Counter and the Ysabel Kid are given in* The Floating Outfit *series' other volumes.*

11 *Told in:* .44 CALIBRE MAN *and* A HORSE CALLED MOGOLLON.

12 *Told in:* GOODNIGHT'S DREAM (U.S.A. Bantam Edition retitled, THE FLOATING OUTFIT) *and* FROM HIDE AND HORN.

With that accomplished, he had been equally successful in helping Goodnight convince other ranchers it would be possible to drive large herds of cattle to the railroad in Kansas.[13]

Having proven himself a first class cowhand, Dusty went on to become acknowledged as a very competent trail boss,[14] a roundup captain,[15] and a town taming peace officer.[16] Competing in a revolver handling competition at the first Cochise County Fair, he won the title, "The Fastest Gun In The West," by beating a number of well known exponents of rapid gun handling and accurate shooting.[17] In later years, following his marriage to Lady Winifred Amelia "Freddie Woods" Besgrove-Woodstole,[18] he became a noted diplomat.

Dusty never found his lack of stature an impediment to his achievements. In addition to being naturally strong, he had taught himself to be completely ambidextrous.[19] Possessing perfectly attuned reflexes, he could draw either, or both, his Colts—no matter whether of the 1860 Army Model,[20] or their

13 *Told in:* SET TEXAS BACK ON HER FEET *(U.S.A. Berkley edition retitled,* VIRIDIAN'S TRAIL).

14 *Told in:* TRAIL BOSS.

15 *Told in:* THE MAN FROM TEXAS.

16 *Told in:* QUIET TOWN, THE MAKING OF A LAWMAN, THE TROUBLE BUSTERS, THE GENTLE GIANT, THE SMALL TEXAN *and* THE TOWN TAMERS.

17 *Told in:* GUN WIZARD.

18 *The members of the Hardin, Fog and Blaze clan with whom we have consulted decline to say why Lady Winifred Amelia Besgrove-Woodstole decided to leave England and live in the United States under an assumed name, "Freddie Woods."*

19 *The ambidextrous prowess was in part hereditary. It was possessed and exploited equally successfully by Freddie and Dusty's grandson, Alvin Dustine "Cap" Fog, who also inherited the physique of a Hercules in miniature and utilized these traits to help him become the youngest man ever to attain rank as captain in the Texas Rangers and one of the finest combat pistol shots of his era: see the* Alvin Dustine "Cap" Fog series *for further details of his career.*

20 *Although the military sometimes claimed derisively it was easier to kill a sailor than a soldier, the weight factor of the respective weapons had caused the United States' Navy to adopt a revolver of .36 calibre while the Army employed the heavier .44. The weapon would be carried on a seaman's belt and not—handguns having originally and primarily been developed for use by cavalry—on the person or saddle of a man who*

improved successors, the 1873 Model "Peacemaker"[21]—with lightning speed and shoot with great accuracy. Ole Devil Hardin's "valet," Tommy Okasi,[22] was Japanese and a trained *samurai*.[23] From him, along with the General's "granddaughter," Betty Hardin,[24] the small Texan learned *ju jitsu* and *karate*. Neither form of unarmed combat had received the publicity they would be given in later years and were little known in the Western Hemisphere at that time. So Dusty found the knowledge a very useful surprise factor when he had to fight against larger, heavier and stronger men.

---

would be doing most of his travelling and fighting on the back of a horse. Therefore, .44 became known as the "Army" calibre and .36 as the "Navy."

21 *Introduced in 1873 as the Colt Model P "Single Action Army" revolver, but more popularly referred to as the "Peacemaker," production continued until 1941 when it was taken out of the line to make way for more modern weapons required in World War II. Over three hundred and fifty thousand were manufactured in practically every handgun calibre—with the exception of the .41 and .44 Magnums, which were not developed during the production period—from .22 Short Rimfire to .476 Eley. However, the majority fired .45 or .44.40. The latter, given the name, "Frontier Model," handled the same ammunition as the Winchester Model of 1973 rifle and carbine.*

The barrels lengths of the Model P could be from three inches in the "Storekeeper" model, which did not have an extractor rod, to the sixteen inches of the so-called "Buntline Special." The latter was also offered with an attachable metal "skeleton" butt stock so it could be used as an extemporized carbine. The main barrel lengths were: Cavalry, seven and a half inches; Artillery, five and a half inches; Civilian, four and three-quarter inches. Popular demand, said to have been caused by the upsurge of action-escapism-adventure Western series on television, brought the Peacemaker back into production in 1955 and it is still in the line.

22 *"Tommy Okasi" is an Americanized corruption of the name given by the man in question, who had had to leave Japan for reasons the author is not allowed to divulge even at this late date, when he was rescued from a derelict vessel in the China Sea by a ship under the command of General Hardin's father.*

23 *Samurai: a member of the Japanese lower nobility's elite warrior class who usually served as a retainer for the Daimyos, the hereditary feudal barons. A masterless samurai who became a mercenary was known as a ronin. From the mid-1800's, increased contact with the Western Hemisphere brought an ever growing realization that the retention of a hereditary and privileged warrior class was not compatible with the for-*

---

mation of a modern industrialized society. Various edicts issued by the Emperor between 1873 and '76 abolished the special rights of the samurai and, although some of their traditions, concepts and military skills were retained, they ceased to exist in their original form.

24 *The members of the Hardin, Fog and Blaze clan with whom we have been in contact cannot, or will not, make any statement upon the exact relationship between Betty and General Hardin. She appears in:* Part Four, Betty Hardin, "It's Our Turn to Improvise, Miss Blaze," J.T.'S LADIES; KILL DUSTY FOG!; THE BAD BUNCH; McGRAW'S INHERITANCE; THE HALF BREED; THE RIO HONDO WAR *and* GUNSMOKE THUNDER.

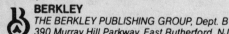

★★★★★★★★★★★★★★★★★★★★★★

The Biggest, Boldest, Fastest-Selling Titles in Western Adventure!

★★★★★★★★★★★★★★★★★★★★

CHARTER'S MOST WANTED LIST

Frank Bonham
_07876-1 BREAK FOR THE BORDER $2.50
_77596-9 SOUND OF GUNFIRE $2.50

Giles A. Lutz
_34286-8 THE HONYOCKER $2.50
_88852-6 THE WILD QUARRY $2.50

Will C. Knott
_29758-7 THE GOLDEN MOUNTAIN $2.25
_71146-4 RED SKIES OVER WYOMING $2.25

Benjamin Capps
_74920-8 SAM CHANCE $2.50
_82139-1 THE TRAIL TO OGALLALA $2.50
_88549-7 THE WHITE MAN'S ROAD $2.50
